LYNERKIM'S DANCE

AND OTHER STORIES

R. H. EMMERS

DOG
SOLDIER

Some stories in this collection have appeared in these publications: "Cowboys and Indians" in *Gone Lawn*; "Crows Always Tell the Truth" in the *Delmarva Review*; "In the Snow Country" in the *Adirondack Review*; "Where Did All the Dentists Go?" in *34th Parallel Magazine*; "Turkeys" in *Streetlight Magazine*.

Lynerkim's Dance and Other Stories

Published by Dog Soldier Publishing

DOG
SOLDIER

The editorial work for this book is entirely the product of the author. Gatekeeper Press did not participate in and is not responsible for any aspect of that element.

ISBN (paperback): 9781662901843
eISBN: 9781662901850

Library of Congress Control Number: 2020939872

For Rosetta, who always stands by me...

CONTENTS

COWBOYS AND INDIANS

They leave us, our lovers, one way or the other. They go to different jobs and new lovers and tenure tracks at universities and high-tech companies and military service and hospitals. Maybe there's a homeless one, as well, selling blood and screaming on street corners, perhaps a crook or two, even a murderer; oh, and some just disappear, their bones shedding flesh until nothing remains.

We were playing cowboys and Indians—one dead already, a neighborhood girl we didn't really know but who came over. Janie was the school marm, Alan a homesteader, me a dead-shot marshal. Alan pretended to die falling from a rock, but it was his collarbone that ended up broken. Later Alan became a minister of the gospel. Blessed be, he told us. We laughed, thinking of that long-ago time he was falling and falling. But he was insistent. Blessed be. Who? Us? I wondered.

When you wander a cemetery, listen while the ghosts tell their stories. They alone never lie. Once upon a time, in the fall, Janie and I lay on a red-checked cloth beside the headstone of an ancestor, gone these many years. There was a picnic hamper with bread and cheese and jam and egg salad and wine. Do you love me? Janie asked. But I did not want to surrender. The sun flickered through the skeletal fingers of the trees. Clouds scudded like fleeing inmates. I nodded and said, Of course. She studied my eyes. Now and forever? she wondered. I sought for an answer.

For a time we lived in an old house on the side of a mountain that leered over a shapeless valley. A path wound down to a stream running through a dark forest which wore many disguises (but never fooled me.) There was one spot beside the stream where the sky appeared; that was Janie's favorite place: fireflies and falling stars. As I sat with her, I tried to decipher what the stream was trying to tell me. Janie was being sickly then, and I would touch her bones and tell her all would be well. Do you think there are some things that can never be healed? she asked me. Was she talking about her illness or something else, I wanted to ask but didn't.

That old house, like something ancient excavated from the sand, or maybe an old photo creased and brown at the edges. (At the time I hadn't yet lost the one of me somber in my Roy Rogers shirt, Janie with a bonnet studying me.) The way the house groaned, whimpering like an old man being summoned for his unknown journey. It made me uncomfortable. One time I even called up Alan, a minister by this time, and asked him the question everyone wants an answer to. What do you want me to say? he told me. We'll all know soon enough. Well, even ministers can have bad days, I suppose.

I remember a cemetery we visited above the fishing village on that last vacation we took. Janie and I watched an old man and an old woman placing flowers. The old man stood and looked out across the boiling ocean and the reckless black sky and said to his companion, Let's get going, if we drive fast we can beat the storm. They went over to their car. And that's how, we learned later, that for a half an hour more they lived on before they too became ghosts. I wondered about the results of Janie's latest tests but couldn't bear to ask.

Janie always liked for me to read stories to her. Pioneers braving the prairies. Ship captains in a storm. Ghosts who appear to their loved ones. No more stories, Janie said to me. I can't bear any more stories that begin and end. But, but, I said. I reached over from the bedside chair and held her as if I were the hammock her bones needed. Janie sighed and looked up at me. Her eyes slowly became a different color.

Having left my lover—an excellent cook, diligent housekeeper and graceful dancer but totally indifferent to those issues which startled me awake in the deepest hours of the night—I decided to return to my childhood home for a period of reflection.

What were these issues that thrust me shuddering out of sleep? No, they had nothing to do with the current Regime, but rather were symptomatic of our modern age in general. For instance, I would suddenly jerk upright in the pitch dark with the overwhelming sense I needed to go to the window, throw back the drapes and reassure myself that the searing moon still hung whole and uneaten in the relentless void of the sky. My lover, awakened by my leap from bed, would sit up, regard me with glaring eyes I could feel boring into my back, and grumble: So what if the moon disappears? Why do you persist in worrying about what you can't change? Didn't Einstein say that was the definition of insanity?

Well, no, but we'll let that pass. (Idiot.)

Oh, you dear and lovely moon, how much longer will you be with us? Will we be granted advance warning of your going, like all the other things we've lost? But about my childhood home. A small white cottage with green shutters, it stood just below the crest of a grassy hill in the middle of a forest clearing. All around was a gathering of heroic trees. Forest creatures great and small gamboled beneath those sheltering branches. How as a youngster I loved to play in that forest where I knew those stately trees would protect me! Grumbling lovers weren't on even the most distant horizon, and heavenly bodies were assumed to be with us forever.

So, homeward-bound it must be.

❏   ❏   ❏

Since my childhood home lay in the most distant part of our dilapidated country, the journey there would be long and fraught: but such journeys should be. As the Bible tells us: *"The path of the righteous is beset on all sides by the inequities of the selfish and the tyranny of evil men."*

The train trundled along the ill-kept rails, rattling and bucking. Passengers swayed back and forth like storm-tossed sailors. Some bore the worried expressions of travelers being propelled into a future they now weren't sure they'd clearly thought out. Others tried to hide smiles; they were the absconders, relieved to be gone. Some passengers were thinking, Oh woe! What is to become of me! While others did all they could to suppress a shout of *Yippee-ki-yay, motherfucker!*

As for myself, I concentrated on rejecting unwholesome thoughts. My new regimen! I was leaving behind those bad times when my thoughts would grow dire, sprouting like dark weeds I couldn't kill no matter how much mental pesticide I'd spray. Those bad times when, realizing with absolute clarity how the disappearing moon would take with it all the light of the world, I would turn to thoughts of the knife. I would imagine the silver mystery of its edge, honed to such an infinite sharpness that it disappeared into itself.

(Sometimes the poetry of the blade would arouse my blood to the point where I'd point at my lover and order, Stay there! Then I'd scurry to the computer and fire up Google to search out images of that exquisite moment when the edge first kisses flesh and draws forth into life that tiny wondrous red bud. Such images were difficult to find, but when I did, my blood would blast through my veins like an IV of cocaine and I would hasten back to my lover, who had stayed in bed as I'd ordered, and we would engage in… Well, I will leave the rest to your imagination. But to ease your mind, no, I never cut a lover, even in fun, except once.)

So, I knew what I was leaving behind and what lay ahead and I was happy about it. I ate my ham-salad sandwiches with contented chomps and filled my mind with the lush and lusty forest of my youth while the brown, wasted scenery of today passed slowly by in the train's filthy windows.

Oh, that forest! My dog Sean and I would wake up long before my parents and set off for a day of adventure. Above us a great tide of brilliant stars would wash across the night sky while the moon gleamed unabashedly. (I assure you, it was like that in those days!) We would hasten out of the clearing where the cottage slumbered and make for our breakfast spot, sheltered in the ample bosom of towering firs, to eat corncakes I'd baked the night before. Then, satisfied and eager, we'd spend our day roaming among the rabbits and the deer and the squirrels and all the other forest creatures who were our friends. Birds we knew would flutter around, telling stories about what they'd been up to. (Stories that were probably made up; you know how birds are. Except crows, who always tell the truth, no matter how uncomfortable. Oh, how much we need the return of crows these days!) When night came again, we'd head home. My parents would already be locked up tight in their room; they might as well have been dead.

That's the way I remember growing up—until I met my first lover and Sean was found dead and I was alone.

❑   ❑   ❑

So, the train carrying me home clattered on. Slowly, of course, the tracks being one more bit of crumbling infrastructure. I often dreamed about infrastructure. After checking to make sure the moon still clung to its precarious perch, I would return to bed and fall asleep only to be pursued by a dream of everything crashing down, highways, bridges, aqueducts, buildings, you name it, all crashing into fiery ruin while I ran frantically about calling out for past lovers—possibly to save them, but I doubt it; more than likely I was seeking one final opportunity for orgasmic release among the bloody ruins. (I will relate more of my dreams later if I have the time but not the really creepy ones.) I would write adamant letters to every politician I could think of, from the Leader on down, demanding action or else there'd be dire consequences. (What these consequences might be, I never spelled out; nevertheless, two Regime agents, one male, one female, paid me a visit. Needless to say, they entered my dreams: as Sean watched, waiting his turn, we frolicked, sometimes the three of us together, other times one on one; how earnest were the howls!)

At any rate, as I said, we were making our slow way west across the vast prairie. During the day, dark storms of high blue wind occasionally raced past, tossing the prairie grass into black teeming waves before the sun blazed again. You'd look out expecting to see a wagon train or a band of wild Indians, but the landscape would be vacant except for the shadows dragged across it by soaring carrion birds. That's the way the boring days went. But the nights! The nights thundered down with a blackness so profound it was like dying and being sealed inside a coffin interred in the blackest depths of the earth. I would sit rigid and guarded, lest I slumber and, awakening, look out at the night sky and find all my worst fears confirmed.

❏ ❏ ❏

You're probably wondering about the other passengers. They were a varied lot, but typical of what you see these days on a public conveyance. Workmen searching for jobs. Brides going to meet new husbands. The usual orphans hoping for new families. Footloose middle-aged women. Dour salesmen with their unsellable wares. A couple sociologists. A prostitute or two. Several expensively clothed middle-aged men with neat haircuts, glittering nails and big bellies, either Mafia dons seeking new territory or hedge fund managers looking for more victims, all of them accompanied by husky young men in bad suits, their bodyguards. I was wearing a disguise, of course, given the possibility that former associates from my time in the drug business might still bear a grudge. From behind the dark glasses that were part of the disguise, I was able to study these husky young men relentlessly, imagining them naked and hot-breathed, bending toward me, wearing their pistols belted around their slim waists. (Of course, I did the same thing with the young female passengers, especially those wearing *hijab* and *abaya*, imagining them naked and sweaty under all those dark, mysterious layers.)

There were many other people in my car, of course, but I won't bother to enumerate them because I'm sure you're familiar with the various types you see traveling these days, always traveling, as if traveling were a substitute for hope. (You'd be familiar with them, that is, unless, you're one of those who has decided to stay hidden for the duration.) Anyway, from behind my dark glasses, I examined the young men and the young women and ate my ham-salad sandwiches and gazed out at the infinite prairie and listened to music on my eight-track. I had many tapes of old-time murder ballads, especially those in which the defiled woman seeks revenge. Revenge is a fundamental human right, in my opinion.

❑   ❑   ❑

And so, the end of our journey was approaching.

Little tickles of arousal jittered through the passengers, either anxiety or eagerness depending upon the reason for the journey: Deathly sick uncle vs. deathly sick *rich* uncle, etc. etc. Several people discoursed into their phones, as people do approaching their destination or calling loved ones in the midst of an air hijacking. Outside, the once barren plain had begun to hump into little pimply hills. In the distance sharper hills rose like cardboard cut-outs against the gray sky. Somewhere over there was my childhood home! Somewhere over there was my forest! Somewhere over there was the body of dead dog Sean!

Across the aisle from me sat a young woman. Wispy hair beneath a blue polka-dot kerchief, plain dress, flinty face, large breasts. She sat upright, looking straight ahead. She was speaking softly, apparently rehearsing a speech. Was it congratulations for some accomplishment? A justification to a parent for outrageous behavior? An apology to a loved one left behind? A suicide note?

No, none of these.

"Dear Theunis," I heard her say, "here is your loving bride Joanna, dispatched to you by the agency after you selected me from the website and sent... No, no, no, wait. How stupid. Okay. Dear Theunis, here before you at last is your eager bride Joanna! How I have longed for this moment through all my long journey..."

I turned away, unable to listen to any more of this drivel. Just shut up and take your medicine, you believer in love! Look, the train will arrive soon at the station and there will be your stout Theunis with his thick ploughman's hands and dim, doughboy face, waiting for the 14-year-old bride he'd ordered, and the two of you will stare at each other as you try to reconcile what you see before you with the image you saw on the internet, and then you will move together into an awkward embrace, subsequent to which you will follow Theunis to his wagon, already filled with supplies, and begin the journey that will take you fifty miles north into the tall-grass wilderness where the lunatic wind always blows and to the sod house where the centipede- and spider-laden dirt drifts down constantly from the sod ceiling into hair and bedding and cook pot and where there is no Wi-Fi and where you, Joanna, will wait until eventually you...

But should I tell Joanna what is coming?

Should I give her the benefit of my experience?

Nah.

❑   ❑   ❑

The anticipatory commotion grew stronger. There were discussions about the best local restaurants and prostitutes. Joanna, across from me, continued her nervous rehearsal. The Mafia dons and hedge fund managers smoothed down their suit jackets and moustaches, their bodyguards checked weapons. The train slowed, lurched. The concrete-block station came into view, its parking lot crowded with cars, trucks and horse-drawn wagons; taxis and rickshaws lined the pick-up lane. Atop the station's slate roof stood a statue of the Leader in one of his patented no-nonsense poses.

As I gazed out the window at this welcome scene before me—my childhood home was just over that ridge to the west! my guardian forest awaited!—my reflection in the glass surged into focus. My face looked haggard from the exhaustion of travel, of course, but seemed still imbued with the good humor I've always been noted for. But wait: another face appeared, then a third, a fourth, a fifth, my face, yes, but all with marked differences. Smiling, leering, eyes rolling, grimacing, laughing, sneering, baring teeth, recoiling in terror!

Was this the way death arrives? In a clown car. Or was I having one more brush with insanity.

Once, back before I set up on my own in the drug business, I worked as chief of staff to the mayor of a medium-size city, privy to all the deepest secrets of his administration, chief among them the fact that he was in thrall to the local crime family, the Gillespie Sisters, who'd ensured his victory with their army of social media trolls and bots. (It also helped that the Mayor's opponent met an untimely death—it was *ruled* a suicide.) After the election, favors were demanded, and I, as chief of staff, was in charge of their fulfillment.

It wasn't a bad job, as jobs involving organized crime go, but I'd entered that phase of life when the nights were a torment. I would close my eyes, sleep would make its hovering approach but then quickly become untethered, spinning away to some remote nook of the universe I knew I could never reach. You might think this was at least in part due to paranoia occasioned by my work with the Gillespie Sisters, but you would be wrong. Yes, I knew many dangerous secrets, any one of which might prompt the Sisters to ensure permanent confidentiality. But the truth is I got along fine with them—we were all three of us oenophiles and Jean-Pierre Melville freaks. There was never a hint of suspicion of me on their part, and we might have continued our relationship for many happy years had they not been assassinated by Regime agents.

No, the paranoia that stabbed my nights like a large, terrifying needle had to do with the fact that I'd come to the sudden realization I no longer knew who I was. I mean I felt as if I were unmoored, floating free, capable of being tossed by even the merest whisper of a breeze, all sense of personal reality brushed away like lint. Was I here on *this* Earth or a different one? Had our universe collided with some parallel universe, in the process sluffing me off into new territory like some errant quantum particle. Had all the accustomed equations been juggled, the cosmological horizon tilted?

Nothing looked different. Everything felt different. I thought I might be going mad.

Of course, one can learn to live with anything, including madness conjured by the Great Physicist in the Sky, as long as one has the loving support of an empathetic partner. Needless to say, I did not, my lover at the time being thoroughly consumed with protesting recent fertility regulations, but I endured, secure in the knowledge that whatever madness this was, another would be sure to take its place eventually and make the current bout nothing but an unpleasant memory.

And sure enough, my worries about the moon soon arrived.

I stood on the station platform with my backpack, breathing air that only moments before had wafted through my beloved forest. How sweet it was in my city-scarred lungs! Passengers milled about, seeking luggage, greeting family and friends, buying fruit from the pushcarts, haggling over taxis or rickshaws. I looked around for the young girl from the train, Joanna, finally spotting her at the end of the platform past the Stuckey's. She was standing in front of a bulky young man with blond hair and a face broad as a shovel, on it a grin: Theunis, of course. He was holding out a sausage-shaped object which after a moment I identified as a pecan roll from Stuckey's. A wedding gift for his beloved he was seeing for the first time! (Jesus!) It was clear what was going on with honest yeoman Theunis—that look of pleased befuddlement at his good luck in scoring a mail-order bride who didn't look or smell like a rhinoceros—but what intrigued me was the string of thought pulses coursing through Joanna's mind. I took out my notebook and wrote down the thoughts I witnessed:

Kiss or handshake?

Why is he grinning like a big Swedish idiot?

Why were Mother and Father killed at the mill?

Could they have saved me if they'd lived?

My life forever, I guess. Unless death. Mine …

Or his.

What is that odor? Oh Lord, is it…?

Is this Love?

Or Fear?

What's the difference? (This was my thought, not Joanna's.)

❑ ❑ ❑

In the Stuckey's I bought an egg-salad sandwich and a pecan roll of my own and stowed them in my backpack, which also contained, among other things, change of underwear, Bible, small revolver, bearer bonds, my childhood stiletto, diary and tin box of opium. While I browsed among the Stuckey's trinkets and striped blankets, I found myself pondering Joanna's situation. It is my observation that the only way two people can come together as partners in this buzzing hive of humanity in which we're all trapped is through the intervention of the Great Physicist in the Sky. It is He who disposes. And how does He do that? According to His own whimsical quantum principles. SNAP! and He has set two lives on course toward each other. The problem is that when they come together, there's a likelihood that, like stars colliding, all that will be left is a black hole destroying all light and time.

When I went back outside with my purchases, I saw stout yeoman Theunis, striding purposefully toward his wagon, Joanna trudging behind as if drawn by a tether.

❑ ❑ ❑

To the west of the train station a low ridge wiggled across the grassy plain. Although it seemed more raggedly eroded and careworn than I remembered—I suppose the same could apply to me—the sight of it warmed me, for beyond that ridge lay my forest and my childhood home. Oh, my friendly forest, waiting to welcome me with your embracing branches and titillatingly barky trunks and smiling, scampering forest creatures. I made my way through the station parking lot, hoping to catch a ride, but I could find no one heading west into the forest. Why should they? What allure did a forest of smiling trees and gaily chattering creatures hold for modern folk immune to magic and governed by the principles of rampant capitalism and quantum mechanics?

This attitude was brought home to me during a conversation with an elderly, pig-tailed gentleman sitting in a rocking chair on the porch of the station hotel, smoking his pipe and reading the Special Prosecutor's Report on his iPad. I asked him if he knew of anyone heading west with whom I might hitch a ride.

You aim to go to the Forest? he said.

I told him I did.

He scrutinized me. Then he said, No, no one goes there. And I would advise you against such a course.

Why?

That place where you want to go?

Yes?

Death is there.

Oh, you crazy old man!

As I set off walking, westward toward my forest, toward my childhood home, I found myself thinking about Joanna. An image kept appearing—so real I might have been wearing VR goggles. There she is before me in the tall grass beside a sod house, standing straight, hands at her sides, serious expression: she's making a speech. Dear husband, here you see before you your bride, Joanna, having traveled to you from the East. She clears her throat. She runs a finger slowly over her lips as if to mold them into an apparatus that can produce the words she believes are required. Dear Theunis, husband, all I ever wanted was for you to adore me, for you to place me above all others, for you to tell me how valuable I am! That's all! And then, we'd stride forward through life side by side, always and forever ...

Husband, damnit, do you hear me?

Well, this is a new Joanna, isn't it?

Then the vision drifts, blurs, dissolves. A new video takes its place:

A low, solitary hill in the middle of the endless prairie, atop it a cemetery. A procession making its way across the grassy plain toward the hill. Men and women in their Sunday clothes, a scattering of children led by the hand or carried at the bosom. In the middle of the procession, a coffin born by a horse-drawn hearse, its driver in a black suit and top hat. Mournful wind. Mournful fiddle music, drum beating a slow, sad march.

The video camera embedded in my brain pans across the scene, then focuses in on the cemetery. Stone markers tilted this way and that, silhouetted against a sky of swirling gray and black clouds. The hearse halts beside a freshly dug grave; a headstone rests against the shoveled dirt. The camera moves along the solemn faces of the mourners, good, solid American faces, then focuses on the headstone. A name is engraved on it.

Theunis Wessels.

❏   ❏   ❏

A few of the things that *might* have killed Theunis:

Disease. Snakebite. Centipede or spider. Accident with a scythe. Kicked in the head by his mule while trying to shoe it. Struck by lightning. Bitten by rabid fox. Drowned in flash flood. Hypothermia after being caught in a blizzard. Shooting accident. Crushed by a wagon that collapsed atop him while he was trying to fix a wheel. Unlucky fall from the roof of his sod house. Prairie fire.

Or..?

❑ ❑ ❑

The gray clouds swirl and the drizzle falls and ladies weep and a hatchet-faced minister preaches: *Listen to me, brothers and sisters! As the eternity of sleep overtakes us, we will be changed! Hallelujah! Brothers and sisters, I tell you it is the greatest mystery! In a flash, in the twinkling of an eye, at the last trumpet! All changed!*

❑ ❑ ❑

Joanna wipes her nose with the back of her hand. She leans against an older woman, the preacher's wife, who supports her with an arm around her waist.

Are we not all sinners? Will not the final trumpet sound for all of us? So seek your Father's mercy before it's too late!

Oh, Joanna, I applaud your performance. As good as anything I ever accomplished.

❑ ❑ ❑

Night after night in her tiny room in the home of her birth, lying on the thin mattress. The white light of a kerosene lamp. The blackness of the sky outside her window. The skeletal hands of an elm wavering across the moon's blotched face. (At least she had a moon!) Night after night in her tiny room reading the magazines, roaming the websites that proclaim love and marriage to be the answers. (But what were the questions!?!) Night after night dreaming, feeling the disappointment of the stern-faced old women in the parlor below seeping up around her like a noxious gas. Night after night. And finally coming across the website for Frontier Brides. Scanning the faces of all the young, handsome, hopeful, solid farmers. Sending in her pitiful savings, waiting anxiously for the response, not daring even to whisper her hopes to the old women in the parlor below sipping sherry and expelling noxious gas.

❑ ❑ ❑

But did Joanna ever let herself gaze up into that night sky? (As I used to do before fear of the moon's disappearance, taking with it all the light, entered my blood like a deadly bacillus.) Did she ever let herself take in the immensity of that heaven soaring beyond the ragged rectangle of sky trapped within her room's lone window?

(As I used to do… Sean and I sitting on a soft carpet of moss beside a stream winding through the forest, and we are gazing up at the billions upon billions of cubic miles of overarching universe, at the billions upon billions of planets and stars and galaxies all spinning onward and outward in their infinite tracks, and we are realizing how tiny a speck we truly are in that gigantic tapestry, and we are understanding finally and irrevocably that whatever we would do with our lives, whatever action we would contemplate, whatever decision we might think needs to be made, all of it would be totally without meaning in that gigantic context. Save a child from drowning, murder a child with a knife, it wouldn't matter because either course would have exactly the same impact on the cosmos.)

❑ ❑ ❑

Joanna watches as the casket is lowered into the muddy grave and the shovelfuls of earth splatter against it. She thinks of those many long months in that sod home while the dirt drifted down and the centipedes and spiders fell into her hair and the winds flamed down across the prairie as if they might eventually shear away all her flesh, all her soul. All that time in the sod house waiting for God to apologize, or at least exhibit some knowledge of her.

So, she took to going out at night while Theunis snored, she would go out and stare up into that infinite sky and wait for an answer, but the only answer was His silence, and His silence stretched on and on as the uncaring galaxies swirled away on their uncaring paths, and at last understanding came to her:

No, it didn't matter what she chose to do.

So, she did it.

❑   ❑   ❑

And there it was before me at last, my forest. I stood at the crest of the ridge amid a clutch of blueberry bushes and took it all in. I felt all the jiggling tribulations and cancerous thoughts of the long train journey from the city to the prairie sluffing off me like dead skin from a snake. Joanna and Theunis? Just some unimportant people who flitted across my peripheral vision as they traveled from one life into another. The hedge-fund managers and Mafia dons with their bellies and $3000 suits and whiskey coughs and bodyguards? I don't know what those words mean. Girls in *hijabs* and *abayas* covering their sweaty nakedness? Begone from my ken!

A breeze wafting through the trees of my forest pranced out to greet me, carrying the pine-oil scent of firs, the honey musk of poplars, the citrus of walnuts. I tore off my disguise. Disgruntled drug customers do your worst!

I longed to plunge into my forest, but I made myself wait so I could enjoy the anticipation. Those heroic guardian trees of my youth, how I remembered them in their stately ranks! Through them we would romp, my dog Sean and I, chasing the little spirited forest creatures who thought it was just a game and we'd never *really* catch them and eat them.

But speaking of poor Sean.

Well, never mind. Sometimes the knife just grows impatient and decides to take matters into its own hand.

❑ ❑ ❑

I have entered my forest.

❑ ❑ ❑

There's something amiss.

❑ ❑ ❑

That clamorous, ugly sound! The trees are shouting at each other. Snarling. Hurling insults and invective. Raising barky fists.

❑ ❑ ❑

My dear forest creatures, what's wrong? There is brawling: maddened bears against maddened bears, elk locking horns, deer tearing each other with razor hooves. The smaller creatures, the rabbits and foxes and squirrels and raccoons, they peer from the shelter of dark thickets with frightened yellow eyes.

Birds are tossed about on angry winds!

Crows black as night sit on branches casting murderous stares.

❑ ❑ ❑

I make my way deeper into the forest, still hoping to reclaim the comfort of my dreams.

But the brambles are thicker and thornier than I remember. It's human flesh they want to feast on! Branches grasp and rake like the skeleton fingers of unrequited old women.

Now there is a sound ahead of me. A thrashing of branches! Angry turmoil!

A great dark creature shows itself. It glides like a ghost among the fronds of the giant ferns.

Wolf? Dog? Mythic creature?

I cup my hands around my mouth and howl a question. The creature cocks its head toward me. It examines me with fierce, shining eyes. Its nose twitches with my scent. Is it remembering?

I howl again. My cry echoes from one tree to another, growing more and more plaintive as it skims the currents, as it dissolves into the mist.

My hands drop to my sides. Suddenly, it's as if I can feel the coolness of a nose nudging my palm. There is actually a moment when I think I feel familiar weight leaning against my thigh. My hand at my side strokes the black fur of a head, a neck.

I look down.

Nothing. Just the emptiness of fouled and departed memory. The emptiness of a ghost creature now gliding away from me through the fronds of the giant ferns.

❑   ❑   ❑

Sometimes I dream I am Sean, that I am still alive, that I am searching through the forest. Then I awake and as I lie there, I find myself wondering if I was a person dreaming I was Sean or if I am now Sean dreaming I am a person clutching a knife.

❑   ❑   ❑

It is night. I have made my way through the forest to the clearing and the bungalow that was my childhood home.

I lie in the bed that was once mine in the small room upstairs that was once my refuge, my cell. The darkness is absolute but I am comforted by the knowledge that I must be surrounded by all my things, my toys, my childhood clothes, my posters…

I hear a sound. What it is and whence it comes are impossible to determine. I leave the warmth of my bed and glide out to the hall-way, careful to make no noise of my own in case it is an intruder bent on mayhem. In the hallway I stand still as death, listening, holding my breath so that I can better taste the currents of the air. But there is nothing further. I strain. Nothing.

Well, I decide, it must have been my parents in their bedroom down the hall. Dead thirty years and still going at it.

Back in my bed, I settle into the warmth of my blankets. On the opposite wall above my desk is the window looking out across the forest. Above the tree line hangs the moon and beyond the moon the stars, all uneaten, all whole, all undefiled.

Of course, I understand that they are nothing more than camouflage hiding the relentless black hole that will someday swallow us all. Maybe even in the next five minutes. Expect an apology from above? Dream on.

I go to sleep with that thought, and Sean stalks through my otherwise worthless dreams.

Then the crows awaken me with their deadly summons.

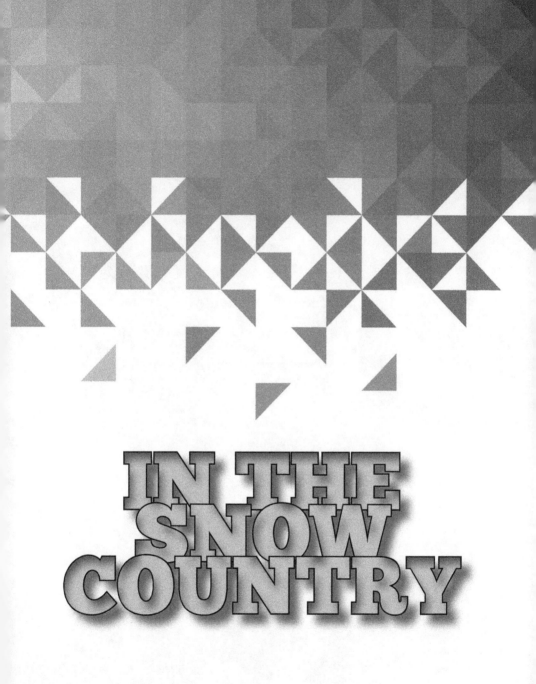

Google said it would be 23 hours and 16 minutes to Superior, Montana. I had to pull over at a rest stop for 44 minutes to make it come out right. I left home after my wife, Jean, died. She always acted so happy and satisfied. Personally, I would have welcomed a few tears—that would have been a sign of hope. We were sitting in the backyard on the new patio set I purchased for her at Sears on the installment plan. She thanked me again for the little gold bracelet. Her white cat climbed our fence and perched atop a post, staring at me as if he were God waiting for me to make a mistake. The sprinklers went thwap-thwap-thwap, silvering the air like a cloud, and I kept waiting for an angel's leering face to peer out and warn of more blessings. I asked Jean to get me a gin and tonic. She brought it in a tall glass, all smiles. Do you see what I mean?

I want to explain about The Plan. The first visit is to be Coeur d'Alene, Idaho, on the other side of the mountains from Superior. School hadn't started yet, and I was home with Grammy. I watched game shows, women with pointed breasts clapping their hands and dancing tippy-toe. I kept turning up the TV, but I could still hear Grammy shuffling around in her room, occasionally pounding on the window to scare away squirrels or demons, I don't know which. The TV flickered like a dying heart. But I felt my blood running thick. I was 17 and still a virgin. Suddenly, Julie Anne was knocking on the patio door. She was a short, fat girl who lived in a crumbling shack in Brush Valley and generally smelled of smoke. Later, after she left and I was back in front of the TV, Grammy shuffled in. She stared at me, squinting with milky eyes. "Are you Jacob? I thought you were dead."

Jacob, my Grandpa, who, denied any hope of further happiness, blew up his own head. I think this had to do with someone Grammy was fucking back then. One day, rummaging through dad's bureau, I discovered a box of rubbers. I opened each crinkly package and took out the rubbers and lined them up like a row of cemetery markers across the top of the bureau. I wasn't sure who would be home first, mom or dad, but either way.

Anyway, Julie Anne now lives in Coeur d'Alene. The Plan specifies that I go there by driving to Superior and hiking over the mountains. I knock on the door and hand her a box. What's in the box? I don't know.

That is the wonder of it all.

❑   ❑   ❑

Superior was right off the Interstate on the banks of a black river, a cluster of crumbling homes urging their last inhabitants to flee. A bridge struggled across the river, and from there the gravel road twisted upward into a forest tormented by snow. By the bridge was a small store with a Nehi sign in the window. The old man behind the counter watched me with eyes as hollow as a snake's as I picked things off the shelves. With a shaking hand, he wrote the prices on a little pad. In the middle of adding them together, he stopped and looked directly at me.

"I hope you know what you're doing," he said. "Up in those mountains, that's a good place for making a big mistake. Then you got to pay the price."

One of those moments occurred. God allowed me to hear what the old man was really saying, and I wanted to kill him right here, stab him in the heart with the knife I'd bought with my other equipment. Knife: 7.35 pounds, blade 4.5 inches long, drop point, S30V stainless steel.

❑   ❑   ❑

An empty white land, as frigid and wasted as that old man's dying flesh. A hollow wind singing to me. At a cabin, deserted for the season, I leave the car, a silver Toyota, 36,647 miles on the clock, fourteen payments remaining. From here on the road is un-plowed, a hard white river. My boots plunge through the crust of the snow. Sometimes I stop and look back, spending long moments studying the holes I've left.

The sky pressing down. The shallow tremor of my heart.

There comes a time when.

All the little dangers of life.

The answer lies deep, some hard icy poison you cannot spit out.

Jean!

❏　❏　❏

I knew what had happened with Julie Anne would be all over school. They'd be passing around notes. They'd snicker and point their fingers and make weird noises like having a convulsion. I kept having a belly-ache, but eventually mom made me go back.

Instead, it was just the same as always. Everyone ignored me as if I were made of see-through rubber. Julie Anne went by, smelling of smoke and with a look like what had happened was all in my mind. But how could I have just imagined sticking my hand down her pants? At any rate, she seemed happy for a change, so I tried to call out to warn her, but the only sound I could make was like a dead bird. (Oh, how things might have been different!) This was almost the end of senior year, and our yearbooks had been delivered. That night while mom and dad squirmed together in the next room, I went through the yearbook picture by picture, picking out all the ones who needed to be part of what was going on. I didn't know it at the time, but this was the beginning of The List.

❏　❏　❏

This country of snow. It falls, burning, from a murderous gray sky.

Crows perched in the dark pines, calling out their secret language.

The heavy pack dragging me down into the weight of the snow.

Why didn't God suggest I bring snowshoes? (He was probably just too busy, off tormenting someone else.)

I sleep in a burrow dug into a snow bank, coiled and dreamless in my sleeping bag. Animals all around me in the wilderness, whimpering like a child moaning in the shadows of his bed while the grownups act out their stupid little desires on the other side of the wall.

Shut up that crying, Paul, or I'm coming in there.

❏　❏　❏

I would crouch in the darkness, watching Jean sleep. The red numbers of the clock face blinked their message. The sheets and comforter were a set I purchased for her at Macy's. But, of course, she wasn't really asleep. She knew how to play the game and never stirred. That's why I loved her.

❏　❏　❏

I worked on The List. First the girls. Julie Anne. Becky Semple, who hung up on me when I called her for a date. Over the buzzing, empty wire after she hung up, I heard her laughing with her friends. I have an address in Huntsville, Alabama. Marsha Hawbaker, who was in my ninth-grade class and one day she throws a book at me. She lives in Scranton, Pennsylvania. There was a girl with dark hair in the corridor by the auditorium after school. I wanted to fuck her so bad. I can't remember how that went, but I can guess. I wanted to put her on The List, but I couldn't remember her name or find her picture. Probably she had adopted a disguise. Of course, I couldn't ignore the boys. It was my job to save them or punish them or something: I hoped it would become clear later. Bill Cronkite. He poured a glass of water on my shoes in the cafeteria. He now lives in Winston-Salem, North Carolina. Robert Nuss. He was first-string tackle on the football team, but that was all I could remember about him at the moment.

It all started in 1992 in Grand Rapids, Michigan. Jean was in college. We went to a party, and at the party she introduced me to one of her professors. I recognized him immediately as someone I'd known for years, a man my father had bowled with. But, of course, he wouldn't admit it.

Soon the professor started running pictures in my head. I don't know where he got them, but after awhile I realized the pictures were actually a storyline I could see unrolling. I would see an event that had happened to me—my father taking me to the bowling alley and introducing me to the professor, for example—and then the storyline would roll on and I would see another event—me meeting the professor at the party in Grand Rapids and him laughing at me. And then the really strange thing is the storyline would keep going on into the future. And there I would meet the professor again, but in totally different circumstances, and learn what resides in God's heart and why He does these odd things.

Currently, there are 63 people on The List. There are those people from the yearbook, Julie Ann and Becky Semple and Bill Cronkite and so on. Then there are other people from various times in the past. The List is people who I have a story about them for whatever reason. I have to visit them and do something. Sometimes I know what it is I'm supposed to do. Marsha Hawbaker from ninth grade, for example. She's the one who threw a book at me. So the storyline is I go to her and slap her cheek, and I'm wearing jeans. She lives in Scranton, Pennsylvania, as I mentioned.

But sometimes I don't know what it is I'm supposed to do when I visit a person. I have a sense, though, that in many cases it involves a price to be paid.

Once I had The List, I had to put together The Plan. I did it on the computer and printed it out. Because the first person on The List was Julie Anne, The Plan specified driving 23 hours and 16 minutes to Superior, then hiking through the pass to visit her in Coeur d'Alene and give her a box. After that, I would disappear until next March. I would have a new identity and travel to Huntsville, Alabama. Then I would just keep going down The List.

Jean and I lived in a neighborhood of arsenic lawns and trees like scarecrows, with kids screaming on their bikes and mothers hiding behind drawn curtains. "You know that yellow house at the corner," Jean said. "The couple that lives there seems very nice. We ought to have them over."

I made one excuse after another, of course. Their faces smiling, their teeth clicking against ice cubes, their heads bobbing, they would have breathed out their sweet, frothy breath trying to woo me. But what I knew I wasn't about to share.

Jean had always wanted a dog, so I got her two, black Labs. They would lie beside the bed at night, ebony ghosts with yellow eyes like distant warning lanterns. When I looked at them, I knew they understood Jean's condition as well as I did and shared my despair. Sometimes, sleeping, Jean's hand would fall to them, stroking their fur. They would moan softly with their terrible knowledge, then grow still again, lying silent, motionless, waiting.

Machinery in the air, the tang of exhaust, a descending thwap-thwap-thwap that swirls cones of snow. By a dark stream running through a grove of naked birch trees that are like a cemetery, I am about to have lunch. Special buffalo-meat jerky fortified with vitamins. I bought it at the same store where, over a period of six months, I purchased the necessary equipment: boots, down jacket, pack, cook set, small gas stove, sleeping bag. There was a large display case filled with knives of all sizes. I finally decided on one that looked like an old-fashioned Bowie knife. The clerk looked at me across the dusty counter. His eyes told me he knew the truth of things. I was no longer alone.

❑   ❑   ❑

The helicopter lands in the snow a hundred yards away.

I wait, sitting on my pack. Two men—a fat young one and an older man with a bristly beard—approach. The fat young one carries a rifle pointed at me. His expression is mournful. They stop ten feet away.

"You was at that store," the older one says. "Down there in Superior."

Chewing, I review it in my mind: Going into the store with the Nehi sign, gathering up some canned goods, the old man behind the counter talking to me as if I were a castaway too insignificant to save, but worse than that. It's like a waking dream, invigorating and portentous and vivid. But suddenly, just as I'm looking at the old man and my hand is reaching for the knife at my waist, the dream goes blank. What happened next? I can only guess.

❑   ❑   ❑

I continued to work on The Plan. The days grew shorter. The trees shed their disguises. Women and men hurried by in sweaters and coats, sullen as refugees. Children cried out their nightmares of ice. But despite my anticipation, the cold winds from the north brought no message.

I took Jean to the lake for a picnic. In the cold we had the place to ourselves. The water lay flat as gunmetal, the feathers of the pines dark on the far shore. I made a fire in the grill. Jean hummed happily as she laid out the food.

I slipped away into the trees. I watched her, studying her silently as she called out for me. Did I detect fear, soft as cancer, on her breath?

There was electricity blue in my veins, and my longing was dark and liquid. You could hear the wind moaning through the dying leaves. When I returned, Jean asked several questions, but never the right one.

Grammy lay on the bed in the dark room. I hadn't seen her around for several months so I decided to take her a cup of cocoa. In the urine-yellow sunlight trickling in after I opened the blinds, I saw that her flesh had fallen away, dry as a dead fish. Only grinning teeth and bone remained to love me and chase away demons. I wept, thinking of Grandpa killing himself because she took up with another man. And now she was dead too. Why did Grandpa kill himself? At first I had guessed it was to destroy the temptation of forgiveness before it could further infect his heart. But as I continued to study the matter, I decided that love had simply become unbearable.

They put handcuffs on my wrists as I finished chewing. Jerky: Buffalo meat, dried cranberries, sugar, sea salt, celery juice, black pepper, red pepper, garlic, onion powder.

"Alright, podner," the older man, the one with the beard, said. "You just come along with us now." His tone was more or less kindly.

The young fat one, the one with the rifle, just stared at me with a quizzical expression, as if he too was hearing pathetic voices in his head but couldn't understand what they were trying to tell him.

❏ ❏ ❏

I would lie beside Jean at night, listening to her breathing, how sometimes it would seem to pause in her throat like she was about to suffocate. The dogs glared at me as if I was supposed to do something. Sometimes I would fall asleep and sometimes I would even dream of how it was when we were first in love, reveling in the lies we happily told each other. But the inexorable loneliness of the bedside clock's ticking would always return me to this world, and once more my heart would pound with its piti- ful desire to be allowed to begin The Plan. But I knew something was missing. I knew my soul remained too cluttered with still- born prayers, despite the hard, pure desire that lived at its core.

I became so immersed in my research and preparations that I lost my job at the printing company. Jean was still healthy and happy at that point. So I continued to leave the house at 8 a.m. I would drive to distant towns I'd never visited before and walk around, looking for people who should be on The List, then return home at 5 p.m. with made-up complaints about people at work. I withdrew a suitable amount from the savings account and told Jean it was my paycheck.

You're probably wondering why I didn't tell her the truth. But you should know the answer to that by now.

❏ ❏ ❏

Days in the air, flying above the snow-covered earth like an angel, the younger fat one sitting across from me. His eyes keep sliding away from mine, from which I take it his wife has left him for someone he thought was his friend.

When we land in the valley, the Sheriff meets us in a patrol car and drives us to the courthouse. He's a gaunt, tanned man wearing cowboy boots and a hat I assume is a Stetson.

"Are we back in Superior?" I ask him.

"Yeah, boy, you're a long way from home."

My home town. The usual: a park with a statue, fire station, police station, post office, red-brick funeral parlor, small shops, doctor's office for pushing needles deep into you, motel with dead bodies behind blinded windows, high school where little girls go screaming down the hallways… Of course, I could go on, but you get the picture.

My cell is on the second floor, up a flight of wooden steps. A large spider crouches in the corner like a messenger. But when, hopeful, I carefully approach, I see it is merely a billow of dust. There are voices downstairs, like parents in another room. Mom and dad enacting their ceremony. Through the keyhole, the wet gleam of light on mom's naked ass, a small constellation of red pimples, a single breathless mole at her waist, dad rooting like an animal, panting and rearing, his whiskers, his clouded breath, his red penis.

The Sheriff drops the cover on the toilet and sits down. "I thought maybe you could use a cigarette," he says, shaking a pack at me. A large gold ring with a blue stone gleams suspiciously on his tanned finger.

"Thank you, sir, but I quit three years ago."

"I want to do everything proper, Paul. So let me ask you, when they arrested you up there on the mountain, you was advised of your rights. Is that correct?"

I try to remember. I don't think the men from the helicopter did any advising, but I want to be agreeable, so I say yes.

"Your right to have a lawyer. Your right you don't have to say nothing to us without a lawyer. But I was sitting down there in my office and I was thinking. Maybe you'd like to talk about what happened."

"It would make a good story if I can get the details in the right order. Sometimes they move around."

"Well, up to you." He stood up to leave.

❑ ❑ ❑

Jean remained cheerful, never complaining, but I was beginning to understand that there is nothing in this world that can ever truly be healed.

I took long walks at night. Up and down the dark streets beneath ghostly, swaying trees, the lights in the little ticky-tacky windows illuminating the crimes being committed within.

Sirens screamed and red lights flashed. But they always saved someone else.

I walked until my legs were like concrete. When I got home, Jean was working on her lesson plan. "Oh, there you are," she said. "Doris from school called and invited us to a cookout Sunday."

Later, in my den, it came to me: Doris must be part of the storyline. Was this the final message?

❑ ❑ ❑

"No, wait, please. I'd like to talk about it."

"This of your own free will?"

"Yes."

"All right, then."

"I remember going into the store for supplies. That old man, I told him I was going up into the mountains and he said, 'Then you got to pay the price.' So whatever happened to him was his own fault. But I just don't remember."

"You're talking about Spangler's store? I want to make sure we have everything correct."

"There by the bridge. A Nehi sign in the window."

"And the old man you mention, white hair slicked back? That's old man Spangler."

"Spangler. That's who I mean. It was his fault what happened."

The Sheriff studied me as his face dissolved and ran off his bones. "Ain't nothing wrong with old man Spangler," he said. "Was him told us where to find you."

From somewhere came laughter. It wasn't the Sheriff; he just kept looking at me mournfully, as if I was his dog and he had to put me down. But the laughter continued. It grew more and more ribald, and that's when I knew it was God offering another of his jokes no one would ever understand.

❏ ❏ ❏

On fall afternoons they went to the stadium and cheered the Nittany Lions. Jean and Paul hugged on a hard wood bench as they held steaming cups of hot chocolate and the ball moved down the field. Jean and Paul, with all their young, raw, hopeful hearts. Could they see what was coming? Did they understand the peril that happiness brings forth?

❏ ❏ ❏

I was 12 years old. My only friend was a crippled boy named Ralph, born with arms and legs that would occasionally jerk out of control into orbits of their own as if he was under the control of a

LYNERKIM'S DANCE AND OTHER STORIES

deranged puppeteer. "Spaz!" they would all shout as he jerked and wobbled down the school hallway.

My dreams? At that time in my life they were consumed by figures undergoing cruel diseases. But the spaz? The spaz dreamed of peddling off on a red Schwinn. Of course, this was impossible, what with hands and feet capable of only irregular contact with the handlebars and peddles and with a body that might bounce off the seat at any moment. But I was his friend. One day I mounted him on my bike. I tied him to the seat with a rope around his waist and told him I'd walk beside him and guide the bike. He squealed with joy! I don't think I need to tell you how this ended. The details remain elusive to me, but I believe that in his short lifetime he had never been happier than at that final moment on the bicycle atop the embankment.

❑ ❑ ❑

But you know as well as I do what had been missing from The Plan.

❑ ❑ ❑

I had already taken the dogs out to the garage. I placed a copy of The Plan on the pillow beside her. Pillow: Kingsize, 34 by 18 inches, 300 thread count, 100% cotton cover, 100% polyester fill, corded.

❑ ❑ ❑

The moon moans through the barred window. Down below, snow falls on the little town sleeping beside the black river as the bodies float by. The Sheriff is gone now. I answered all his questions, told him all my secrets. "And then?" was the last question he asked.

"The end result is there. I spent the rest of the time in the garage playing with the dogs."

❑ ❑ ❑

None of you who haven't been here really knows what love requires.

WHERE DID ALL THE DENTISTS GO?

One morning after we'd been together eight years, Miss D announced that we must flee the city. This notion, she said, had assailed her dreams over a period of some weeks, and indeed she had recently seemed pensive and distracted. I enjoyed living in the city, especially given the easy access to material, blackmarket and otherwise, for my project, but Miss D, whose dreams could be forceful indeed, was adamant. Can you not see what's happening? she said. Escape is necessary! She rarely employed exclamation marks, but when she did I knew better than to contradict her.

But escape to where? Miss D began to take long, rambling trips on her motorcycle, camping out, often gone weeks at a time, and it was during one of these excursions that she came upon M..., which, she told me later, did not appear on any of the maps she carried nor was it recorded by her several GPS devices. She spent an afternoon walking the streets and alleys of M..., after which she determined it was the place to escape to. Why? I asked.

It may appear my coming upon M... was accidental, she replied, but I do not believe so. The couple who adopted me from the orphanage were physicists of a sort and taught me that the universe is full of mysteries, one being that what might appear to be a chance encounter generally isn't. Which I believe applies in this case, M... being just the sort of place of escape I have been seeking. Two other points recommend it, she added. Number One, as I was walking about, I saw many people, but none of them inquired into my business. Bravo! Privacy is to be cherished any day, but these days especially.

Number Two? I prompted. Number Two, she said, no children.
None at all. I started to ask about this, but she abruptly walked
away to find the tool she needed to help the super fix the elevator
in our ancient, crumbling apartment building. So, the village of
M... it was. We left behind the clamorous city of my birth—whose
noise, scurry, and frequent riots had never bothered me, just the
opposite, in fact—and set off across the prairie for the village that
was to be our blessed home going forward. It was an afternoon
of blazing sun and hard blue sky that hurt the eyes. Through the
chest-high grass the billowing wind cut dark stampede trails

Buffalo, I said to Miss D. She was looking all around with that
penetrating gaze of hers flaming through the thick lenses of her
goggles. I don't know if I ever told you this, she said, but sometimes I dream I'm a Sioux warrior chasing bison on a rugged pony
with my flint-tipped arrows and painted face. No, you never told
me, I replied, but I wish you had.

Miss D nodded. We might be better off these days, she mused, if
there were more Sioux warriors on the scene, given the number of
people who should be scalped, but all the Sioux, their hope for the
future dead, took that last, long ride west many, many years ago.
They understood how things work.

❑   ❑   ❑

M... was in the middle of endless grasslands many, many miles
west of our former city. On our arrival the general impression I
acquired was one of bedragglement and ennui. Sagging buildings,
fly-specked windows, empty store fronts, dusty streets. The wind
carried the aroma of dust and the ghosts of cowboys and Indians.

Present-day men and woman were sitting on benches along the
sidewalk, in general bearing the bland, unfixed gazes of people
who've been in a waiting room too long. A number of these people
were holding up newspapers which they might or might not actually be reading. The only headlines I could make out concerned

going-out-of-business sales. There were no boys riding bicycles with baseball mitts hooked to their belts nor any little girls squealing about frogs; as Miss D had noted, this village had no children. A few people were walking around but didn't appear to be headed anywhere in particular, just passing time. A train sat supinely at the station, the track ending some little distance ahead of it. A young woman leaned from an upstairs window while a gingham curtain billowed sadly around her, and from this it was clear she pined for someone who had left her.

Although I was a bit worried about finding the necessary parts for my project, the state of the village didn't bother Miss D. Rather, as she carefully examined what in my view were our dilapidated surroundings, she would express her satisfaction with a variety of sotto voce comments. Oh yes. No need for pretense. Just as I hoped. Indeed, our arrival seemed to have restored her normally sanguine mood. Now she examined everything with wide-eyed glee and pointed at this and that with childish wonder. The pining woman especially intrigued her. This was, I assumed at the time, because she had studied most of history's strange disappearances such as those of William Cantelo, Wallace Fard Muhammad, Joan Risch, Ambrose Bierce, and Cotah Ramaswami. And, as she pointed out, those are just the ones we hear about because they are famous. There are many, many more. It is possible, she added, that this phenomenon has something to do with parallel universes, which, as you know, I have been studying. But I believe something more fundamental to be the cause. That pining woman, for example. What does the expression on her face tell you? I was about to comment, but Miss D held up her hand for quiet and pointed to a house.

It was an old house of two storeys with a tower, set off by itself on the south edge of the village. In front of it was a large, drooping tree, a weeping willow, which seemed fitting. This was because the house looked to me as if it was quivering in despair and might fall down at any moment. Its windows were sightless, its doors should have been hung with exit signs. I was about to convey this impression to Miss D, but I saw she was already enthralled. I should have known. Collapse and ruin had always enticed her.

We soon learned that the owner had departed two years ago, leaving no heirs or instructions regarding the property. Just as I suspected, Miss D said. Thus, we shall take possession. As I said before, when Miss D set her mind on something there was no turning back, so take possession we did.

We began to furnish it with items found at the area's abundant garage sales. This was because Miss D preferred old things; also there was nothing new for sale in M... Meanwhile, we lived in a conical tent beside the weeping willow, Miss D's idea. We live on a prairie, she explained; we should embrace it. Literally, she added sternly, and showed me the posture she deemed appropriate. Some day, she told me as we flattened ourselves on the grass, fingers digging into the soil, it may be useful, for you especially, to have something to hold onto.

What our neighbors thought of this behavior, I do not know, because generally we were only aware of them as eyes peering through briefly parted curtains. But one afternoon as I came down from my tower workshop, I found Miss D in discussion with a woman. I gathered, presently, that this woman was on her slow way home after walking downtown for a teeth-cleaning appointment with her dentist only to discover him gone like her last dentist and the one before that, the office deserted and boarded up. Heading home, she had seen our tent and stopped by on the off-chance it had something to do with departed dentists. Miss D had informed her, however, that the tent had nothing to do with dentists but rather was meant to invoke Indians and buffalo, symbols of which she had painstakingly painted on the canvas. Of course, Miss D added as an afterthought, it is true that the Sioux and buffalo did disappear, so in that sense, at least, they are like your various dentists.

Oh, I see, the woman was saying to Miss D as I approached. This woman was a dried-out woman with features scoured into sharp edges by what I assumed was the cutting prairie wind. It was obvious she had been destroyed by love and now, dreams gone, was just waiting for the moment when she could let herself be carried away by that wind. In fact, she was just now explaining to Miss D that she once had a boyfriend, a fine-looking fellow who was pursuing his dream of selling Bibles door to door but was finding it difficult since everyone in M… already had a Bible and boxes of abandoned Bibles filled the basement of the deserted church. Then one day, the boyfriend was no longer there. Gone, totally (although for a long time she imagined she could still see his shadow). And now the various dentists gone too, now and over the years. I'm thinking maybe I should… she started to say but saw me coming and scurried off with a horrified look as if she had just been confronted by an ax-murderer.

Yes, her boyfriend's shadow, Miss D said to me later. Lost love is like that. The look in her eyes told me not to inquire further.

❑ ❑ ❑

The day came when we could move into the house. Miss D was a whirlwind, planting flowers and decorating the shrubs with ancient artifacts she'd acquired during her years in Southeast Asia. (She thought about placing her 1946 Indian Chief with skirted fenders in the middle of the yard as additional adornment but decided against this, she told me, because the motorcycle had an unfortunate tendency to roam by itself. Afraid it might decide to follow the Sioux, she confined it to the shed.) When she was done in the yard, she summoned me from my tower where I was working on the emergency kill switch for my project. (It turned out my worries about finding the necessary parts in M… were unfounded; the village, unsurprisingly, was replete with junk yards.) As we stood admiring our old house, I congratulated Miss D. A capital job, I told her. Everything is now complete! Of course, I wonder if we could talk about…

No, she replied, children would be a distraction. They have dreams, you see, and they're always chattering about them and the wonderful life ahead. Ha! I am reconciled to the way things are, which includes you. I do want to note here that I rated our marriage as more or less satisfactory, given the current state of things and despite the issue of children and a couple of other things. Generally, I felt a measure of fondness for Miss D and I believe she felt likewise toward me. Of course, there were also those times when I would want to… But that is a whole different story involving why I started my project. Suffice it to say, working with my hands on my project and thinking about the day it would be completed always saw me through those trying times when I would want to…

Anyway, Miss D now decided to make certain alterations to the house: a deck, a gallery, a gazebo, bigger kitchen. We might as well be comfortable while we are here, she pointed out. I voiced my encouragement. After all, I had my project; why shouldn't she have hers? Without another word, she set off toward the center of the village where we had seen all the people sitting around or walking aimlessly or leaning out of windows. Such a small village, but so many layabouts! Miss D and I had discussed this after we had made our initial inspection of M…

Why are they all here? I had asked. I had assumed Miss D was thinking the answer might have something to do with mul-tiple universes, a favorite topic of hers, as I pointed out ear-lier. I knew she had been studying the villagers and I wondered what conclusions she was reaching. I could imagine her brain working away. I could almost see the equations tumbling through it as if propelled by a leaf blower. (She was, by the way, in the pro-cess of repairing ours.)

But all she had said was, Why are we here?

At any rate, Miss D, having gone in search of labor for her projects, returned with a skinny young man. (My first thought when I saw him was that he needed pancakes but Miss D prepared pancakes only on certain holidays.) Shortly thereafter, a sputtering truck arrived and deposited piles of lumber scavenged from deserted homes. That afternoon, the skinny young man began to build a backyard deck to Miss D's specifications.

Meanwhile I continued work on my project, the wiring for which was nearly complete. Downstairs Miss D puttered away on the collection of discarded small motors she was rebuilding. At least once a day we would come together in the backyard to check the progress of the deck and to examine the weather trampling across the endless prairie upon which the village of M... cringed. The deck progressed but the weather remained the same: the vast bowl of the sky a deadly blue while beneath it moaned a tireless, unforgiving wind that exhausted the ears. I had been noticing Miss D's mood changing again; perhaps it was this surly weather.

The skinny young man, maybe hoping for platters of pancakes, had managed to sink pilings and lattice them with cross members. Now planking had begun to appear. Miss D pointed out a corner which she said would be perfect for her telescope, the lenses for which she had begun furiously grinding as if she had set a deadline for herself. After a time, the deck was half completed. Miss D and I spent an evening on this finished section engaging in a poetry duel. She won, of course.

There in the starless dark, the poise, the hover, There with vast wings across the cancelled skies, There in the sudden blackness, the black pall Of nothing, nothing, nothing—nothing at all.

I should have known the answer, of course, but could not summon it. Before she could hide it, I saw the stony look on Miss D's face. What was going on with her?

But I couldn't worry about that; I had to focus on my project.

The next morning, the skinny young man failed to arrive. The absence of hammering enveloped us, a forlorn emptiness.

We waited.

Nothing.

The skinny young man had quite disappeared.

I expected as much, Miss D said, and proceeded to walk downtown where, she told me later, she peered at passersby and through the foggy windows of bars, stores, and offices even though many of them were closed and abandoned, in search of another workman. Their ranks, she found, were sadly diminished.

She did arrive back home, however, accompanied by an older man with his hair in a ponytail. As they crossed the lawn, they were arguing about the Rosenbergs. I quickly fled upstairs to work on my project, the subject of the Rosenbergs being one of those I always avoided around Miss D: she could become exceedingly overwrought! (Their poor children! she would exclaim. Too soon deprived of their youthful hopes!) But she and the ponytailed man seemed to be getting along fine.

At any rate, I soon heard a hammer once more banging away. From my tower, I watched the ponytailed man busily working away at completing the deck. But I noticed that every so often, he would pause in his work and gaze off to the west, across that wind-rippled prairie that traveled on and on to the end of the world. Was that where the disappearing people had gone?

I thought this would be an interesting topic to discuss with Miss D, but she had gone to the hardware store, which was having a going-out-of-business sale, in search of a piece to repair either her telescope or the toilet. (I hadn't quite heard her clearly.) So, I locked the door of my work room and went down to the ponytailed man. He took one more whack at a nail and laid the hammer aside. There, he said wearily, this here deck be finished.

Well, I said, a good job indeed. So, what do you make of all these disappearing people?

He stood in somber thought. His face was lined, eyes sun-bleached. His big, wide teeth were so densely packed it was a wonder he was

LYNERKIM'S DANCE AND OTHER STORIES

able to force words out from behind them. What do I make of it? he said after a moment, speaking slowly and with obvious effort—oh, those stout teeth! It's like I told your missus: people come here for a reason. Then they gotta make up their mind. Maybe it takes 10 minutes, maybe it takes 10 years, y'know?

Make up their mind? About what?

The ponytailed man looked at me as if I were a dolt. Why, he said finally, in an exasperated manner, it's because they got choices! There's the Midnight Movers, but that's pretty expensive. Or the Society for Vanishing, maybe The Way to Elsewhere Cooperative. And, of course, some are do-it-yourselfers, like your workmen…

I thought a moment. But where do they… I started to ask.

You don't know nothing, do you? he replied and gave me another exasperated look. Then he picked up his tools and trudged off to begin work on the front porch that Miss D had determined would be the next project to enhance our old house.

Two days later, the front porch unfinished, the ponytailed man was gone.

❑　❑　❑

And that's the way it went.

Miss D would walk down to the center of M… She would return with a likely candidate from the diminishing numbers available. There would be hammering, sawing, drilling, etc. etc. etc. Then the activity would abruptly cease. The front porch, for instance, was finished by a fat man with a limp who then went to work on the gazebo Miss D thought would add a grace note to the backyard. He was there hammering away when I looked down from my tower at noon and gone when next I looked down at one o'clock. Then there was a young man with a club foot who was set to work finishing the gazebo; he was nearly finished when he too was simply gone.

Yes, that's the way it went.

It was baffling.

One evening as we were sitting on the deck waiting for Venus to rise—this being one of those times when the planet glowed especially brightly, Miss D's spirits were better than they had been for some days—I raised the issue. These men who came here and worked and then just didn't come again, I said. Do you ever see them on your visits downtown?

No, Miss D said, concentrating on the complicated equations she was trying to solve on her iPad, they've chosen to go, of course.

But why? I continued. Where are they going?

Miss D looked up with annoyance. You really don't know? she said.

I told her I did not.

She studied the computer screen, pondered, made a notation, started to say something then thought better of it. A habit of hers I found particularly annoying.

❏ ❏ ❏

The days passed. Miss D continued her treks downtown, returning with more vanishers, a category that now included women. Generally, they made a pretense of working on various parts of the old house, but pretty much nothing of value was accomplished before they went off to... wherever it is they went off to. Meanwhile, I was proceeding with my project. What joy I felt, as I began to fit the pieces together, screwing screws, soldering electronic parts. At last my life would be complete! My woes banished!

At any rate, I was so busy I had little time to spend with Miss D. But finally the day came when I soldered the last little diode into place. Done at last! Eager to hear Miss D's reaction, I leaned out the window of my tower and saw her below in close, animated conversation with a stout woman leaning on a cane. I hurried down and found Miss D alone. I looked all around but all I could see was a trail heading off through the tall grass, empty and endless, dissolving into the far horizon.

I walked a little way along the trail, thinking I might discover some clue, but there was nothing.

I returned, ready to ask Miss D about it, but she was walking away toward the house.

When I entered the parlor, she was sitting on the sofa, pouring tea from her silver Iranian samovar into delicate bone china cups decorated with mythical beasts. Her favorite Beethoven sonata, the 23rd in F minor, played by Gieseking, was on the gramophone she had built. She set out the cups, then leaned back and closed her eyes.

I sipped the tea, then set down my cup. Miss D, I said, I would like to discuss something.

Her eyes remained closed.

Your project? she said. Your new diet? The role Of Tiresias in The Wasteland?

No, I replied. What is bothering me is the people who disappear. So I want to ask you again: why do they come to M...? Why do they then go away? Where do they go? What is the answer?

Several moments passed. She still did not open her eyes, but a tiny smile tickled her lips. I wondered if she had perhaps fallen asleep and was dreaming of things to break so she could repair them.

Buffalo? I ventured. The end of the world? Things breaking? Sioux warriors?

She murmured something I could not make out. I leaned close. Her lips moved again. Very softly, she explained it all to me.

I sat back. Yes, of course.

As she watched me, the tiny smile reappeared, a tiny mocking smile.

Mulling all this over, I went to the gramophone to turn over Mr. Gieseking. I heard the closing of the door. When I turned back, Miss D was gone.

I called out but received no answer. I waited to see if I would hear the sound of her motorcycle, but there was only an immense, annihilating silence all around.

Yes, she was indeed gone.

But all's well that ends well, I suppose.

From my work room upstairs in the tower came a long rattle then a drawn-out yowl and finally a soft, conciliatory entreaty. The sound was perfect. In my opinion, there is no emptiness that cannot be filled—with something.

BLUE WIND

A storm tramples the prairie, blots the sky. No escape from the relentless blue wind. The house shakes, defending itself. The ancient barn trembles, wishing it was elsewhere. The corn fields cringe.

Then the storm passes, galloping east to rage against someone else.

Josie stares out her bedroom window. The horizon, so many millions of miles away, is a knife in the heart.

The storm's darkness had enveloped her. As it passed it tried to snatch her soul. The blue wind is like that; it disappears things.

❏   ❏   ❏

How indistinct, that line between dream and memory. The time in the desert, in the Bentley convertible, her blonde hair flaring in the breeze? Some garbage-strewn alley with the tip of the spike poised at her vein? And this: lying on a blue blanket spread on the grass beside a stream, her yellow sundress pulled off one shoulder, breast waiting and expectant, moist eyes staring up at me?

Baby, she whispered to me. Oh, baby...

❏   ❏   ❏

Are you really anything more than your legend? There was a guy, a boy, you know who I'm talking about, he grew up on a farm near her, just down the county highway in fact, a tough little guy, that's how everyone thought of him anyway, he got out of there and went to work for a local moving company in the city and one day Alfredo, the owner, asked him to do a special job, five hundred dollars, take care of some guy.

But I was talking about her, Josie, wasn't I?

❑   ❑   ❑

School was an hour away on the bus. Each of us standing at the end of our own farm lane, we'd wait for the bus, even in winter when the insolent wind hurtled beneath a sky white as newly scraped bones. There was a boy Josie had lunch with every day in the cafeteria, a year older. Were they in love? I don't know. He would talk about his dreams, and when he did, Josie would study him with a perplexed look, as if his voice was coming from somewhere else. Then that boy was gone, he couldn't wait, he moved to the city and got a job and one thing led to another, he became memory, dream, he became legend. Josie lingered. But everyone is captured eventually. One early morning in May, two months after her 18th birthday, while everyone was asleep, she wrote a note to her parents.

In the dream I watched her counting the money, $302, she made helping her sister clean the Lutheran church, writing the note to her parents, hitching to the bus terminal in the city, buying a ticket to Denver. She wonders if there is a part of her that can still be born. I wonder if she remembers that day beside the stream. On the bus she sits beside an old black woman who keeps whispering out her secrets, one after another: God fucked me once; after that last episode I had to get rid of her; those pills, they cut you right down the middle; nothing can be healed. And the sullen prairie unrolls, brown and endless, occasionally consenting to farms that look abandoned and villages that seem beyond caring. But it was as if everything was instantly and strangely erased after they had passed by. All gone. Then, like a miracle, the city's ramparts. Josie goes to the rest room at the rear of the bus. When she comes back to her seat, they're pulling into the Greyhound Terminal. After they get off the bus, she rummages in her bag for money to buy a hotdog. All gone, all the $302! She runs outside. The old black woman who'd sat beside her on the bus is getting into a cab. As the cab speeds away, the woman turns and through the back window offers a sad smile, like the onset of a terminal illness.

❑　❑　❑

Time passed, a month, a year, a century. I was drinking at the Spur in Billings when a Shoshone cut a guy's face with a knife and had to take off. We ran into each other from time to time after that. His white man's name was Mike. We rode our bikes to Glendive and got drunk and scored some oxy and Mike said he was tired and going back to the res and I knew he too would be only dream or memory. (In the years to come I would sometimes call myself Mike or Michael, in his honor.) Then one day in Denver Josie, who'd been living on the streets, went to the Sally to take a shower. She'd been sending postcards back home telling them how great she was doing. Dear Folks, I'm saving lots of money so I can go to cosmetology school. But she felt like a shadow, a dimness she couldn't grope through, a disturbance in the air that wouldn't pass. Michael was at the Sally to see if any new information had come in about this guy he'd once met in Billings, they'd ridden their bikes all over Montana, he'd lost touch but now wanted to do some business with him. When they were having coffee, he told Josie he'd been working as a cook at the Terminal Bar but recently got fired due to a misunderstanding involving the cash drawer and was now considering his career options. They drove deep into the mountains on Michael's motorcycle, up through clouds, up above the earth, up above everything! Michael muttered in a strange language, Shoshone, he explained to Josie, the words a prayer of acceptance of the world and all that it contained. This made Josie think. She said, How does that work? Be the eagle, Michael said, and pointed to the tattoo on his shoulder. (It was in Helena that we each got tattooed.)

And so, Michael did some business and after awhile they could afford a room above a pawn shop on Larimer Street. One night Michael said he had to go to Littleton to meet this guy. A week later a body was found in a drainage ditch near the South Platte, throat cut from ear to ear.

❏ ❏ ❏

Josie disappeared from me. This was probably the period of time during which she got her own eagle tattoo on her left wrist. It was also during this time that she began using the name Josie Michaels, with an ID to match. Everything else that occurred during this period is available for you to imagine.

❏ ❏ ❏

Time rolled by, a decade, a century, but always a blur, our lives in and out of focus. Reno, Spokane, Boise, Tacoma and so forth. Josie showed up in Salt Lake. Having been involved in several incidents of shop lifting (I remembered her fondness for Little Debbies) and disorderly conduct, she was serving time in juvie. At the juvie camp, another girl became offended when Josie smiled at her and this girl and two others beat her up and raped her in the garbage shed behind the barracks, resulting in various injuries. But, as I am often reminded, that's why God gave us oxy, codeine tablets and various other drugs, so that I could sell them to the guards at the juvie and elsewhere who in turn sold them to the inmates. Eventually, Josie was placed with a foster family. Dear Folks, Sorry for being out of touch, cosmetology school has just been real busy. A good Mormon foster family. They ate dinner at 5:30 exactly and would only allow one hour of TV a day. You'd watch them trooping to their temple in all their best clothes every Sunday. They had a baby daughter. Josie would spend hour after hour just sitting there, staring at that pink sleeping creature and imagining all kinds of outcomes, some good, most bad. They also had a son who was 14 and kept trying to feel her up. Oh, how Josie wanted to love this family! She had learned there was value in being a shadow but longed to be a shadow in this family's embrace! (They gave her an allowance and it, combined with what she stole from the petty cash jar, was available for oxy from the local dealers.) But a month after she arrived, they told her she'd have to have the eagle tatt removed because it was an offense to God and a constant reminder of her mistakes. They made no mention of Josie's sometimes odd behavior occasioned by the oxy or, for that matter, the money missing from the petty cash jar. (Perhaps this had something to do with the mother's fondness for Adderall.) Regardless, Josie ran away, hitched a ride, survived an adventure involving a woman and a crippled dog escaping from her pimp, and eventually arrived in Vegas.

She was panhandling on Tropicana Avenue. A man on a motorcycle stopped and gave her a dollar. He took off his dark glasses and gazed intently at her. When he spoke, she heard Michael's voice once again. She got on the back of the motorcycle and rode off. He said his name was Ephraim, but Josie knew better. He lived in an RV in a campground in North Vegas to save money. He was a dealer at a low-end casino off the Strip but planned on working his way up. After she took a shower at the RV, they went to Wal-Mart for clothes, etc. etc. etc. Pleasant days. Dear Folks, Things are good, will try to get home when I can. They often rode out into the desert. To Josie the sun there, always straight up for some reason, seemed kind: it didn't like shadows. There was a small oasis surrounding a cool, clear pool. Josie liked to lie naked on a warm rock and stare up into the sky. (There's an eagle soaring above her, riding the currents, floating like a dream, and Josie's soul leaves her body and flutters upward to ride the blue currents beside the eagle and, oh, there were so many times I imagined I was an eagle and could catch her and fly away with her.)

But then one day two men in suits came to the RV and took Ephraim away in their Cadillac. When they returned him six hours later, his face was battered, an eye was swollen shut and bruises covered his body. As Josie held him, he wept. Between sobs, he explained that he was in too deep and if he didn't come up with more money, the men would smash his fingers to pulp with a hammer. What did the future hold for a dealer who couldn't use his fingers? Please help me. Anything, Josie said. So Ephraim started bringing men to the RV, sometimes two or three a day. But the money wasn't accumulating quickly enough. The solution was for Josie to work the streets downtown.

The whole demeanor of the man who said his name was Ephraim changed with the threat to his fingers. He stormed at Josie to work harder. She exhausted herself patrolling her beat. One night when she met Ephraim with just $200, his dark rage exploded. Fucking bitch! he screamed and bounced her head against a car window. Then his fevered (and threatened) fingers were around her neck. Only after she'd passed out did he recoil in horror. Two days later a white Bentley pulled to the curb beside her. I rolled down the passenger window and beckoned her closer. She was hesitant, of course. She studied me. I was wearing an expensive suit, my beard and hair were trimmed, my nails fresh from the salon. I could see all of this registering on her. A faint breeze lifted her blonde hair. A fingertip touched her lip. That yellow sundress slipping off her shoulder, that day beside the stream when she said... She opened the door and slid onto the pale leather of the passenger seat. I often think of that yellow sundress, I don't know why. We drove across the desert, her hair flaring in the wind of our passage. We were escaping. That day beside the stream... Oh, that lost place of the heart.

Haven't you ever had a dream so real it's like a memory?

It was a black Cadillac that pulled to the curb beside her. The driver was an older man with a nice suit, a fresh haircut, beautiful fingernails. At the motel, in his moment of jubilation, he cried out Dear Jesus, my Savior! Then he lighted a cigarette. Through the veil of smoke, he eyed the girl. He thought, Jesus, she's so young, as young as my daughter. But God, what a fuck! And Josie? What *was* she thinking about? That little pink baby, how old would it be before it knew if it was going to be happy or sad?

They left the glittering city in the big black Cadillac. The chilled air from the dash blew against Josie's face like a long-awaited kiss. The desert slipped past as the long carpet of highway unrolled into what Josie understood would be her future. Dear Folks, she longed to write, I've met a very interesting man and... They stopped at a little desert village with a giant thermometer so the man could buy gas. He bought her coffee and a pack of Little Debbie cakes. She gave him a blow job. He again shouted his thanks to the Blessed Savior. Again, he lighted a cigarette and through *this* smoky veil watched Josie as she wiped her mouth. Then he blinked, and then his eyes slowly closed, it was as if he could no longer bear what he was seeing. Josie just smiled.

❑ ❑ ❑

All these memories, these dreams...

The yellow sundress...

❑ ❑ ❑

The man driving the black Cadillac, Harold, owned a wholesale wine and liquor business. It was a business of long hours and various pitfalls, and to relieve his tensions he would drive from LA to Vegas to visit strip clubs, brothels and massage parlors. One of Harold's best customers was a man named Eddie Zavarian who owned several restaurants and bars and a club called Venus. On his trips to Vegas Harold occasionally came in contact with young women he thought would be assets at Eddie's Venus club. He even brought several of them back to LA and introduced them to Eddie. Harold did not view himself as a pimp; rather he thought he was doing these girls a goodness by getting them off the streets. At any rate, the black Cadillac eased to the curb two blocks from Venus.

Harold gave Josie all the money in his wallet, $302, and one of his business cards, on the back of which he'd written a note. Then he drove away. Eddie Zavarian sat in his big leather chair in his office and silently studied the handwritten note on the back of Harold's card. He studied Josie with his small bright fat man's eyes. Then, still without speaking, he nodded and pressed a button on his desk. A burly man entered and took her away to one of the small apartments Eddie rented to his girls.

Josie was well received by the Venus customers because she was a New Girl. (As we sat around the stage, our eyes shone with a desire that was less about lust than a yearning for that which we had lost.) Nebraska is far, far away; there is no memory of wind. Dear Folks, Cosmetology is great, I love the way people smile at me when I've done a good job.

But the work is exhausting. The Venus girls work ten-hour days, often six days a week. They dance on the big stage and then move to one of the dark alcoves behind the stage for the negotiation of lap dances and other favors. This process is repeated seven or eight times a shift. The customers are never bothered by the girls' odor of old sweat and baby powder. Nor are they bothered by the pretend smiles. They just want the reminder of flesh. Josie has become friends with one of the other girls, Naomi. I hate their foul breath, their greedy hands, their… Josie is telling Naomi during a quick break between sets. Oh God, if I could just… But I'm so tired. She starts to cry. Naomi takes her into the bathroom and shows her how to survive. The smoke is creamy, butterflies in the blood, flickering fireflies in the heart, the ringing of delicate bells, it's euphoric, rapturous, in twenty minutes she wants another hit, she takes the small white chip of a rock from Naomi's palm and adds it to the pipe, the high grows and grows, Josie's skin vibrates like a tornado, Xanax from Naomi evens things out.

❑ ❑ ❑

Josie moved in with Naomi so they could save money. Whatever they saved they spent on smoke, it made the groping hands and beady eyes bearable. An amount of time passed. Eddie Zavarian watched with a sad half-smile, he knew what was coming, he'd seen it all before. Heroin was better than Xanax for smoothing the rough edges. La Buena, White Lady, Big Nurse, Smack, Skag, all the lovely names we adore. Whatever the name, these girls were Walking with the King! Over the next many months, a year, a century, whatever, Eddie watched with that same sad smile as they zombiefied, sinking day by day, growing thinner, losing the illumination of the eyes, it was what it was, Eddie thought, except they weren't really attracting the customers anymore, and it was a customer-driven business, after all.

One morning at 4 Venus was shutting down, exhausted dancers disentangling from the last few customers, trooping wearily back to the tiny dressing room. Josie went into the bathroom and dried the sweat with paper towels and vomited into the toilet. She stood against the sink and looked into the cracked mirror and saw... nothing, her reflection had fled. Alphonse the burly bouncer was waiting for her in the dressing room, he had hold of Naomi's arm, she sagged against him as if her bones had melted, he took Josie's arm in his other hand. You gals ain't been keepin' up the rent, so I'm taking y'all to your new home. This was a room with peeling wallpaper and a cracked linoleum floor above one of Zavarian's several massage parlors. The first thing they did was get out their stash and do up. Josie fell back against the stained sofa. The syringe fell in her lap. She stared at a small crucifix a previous tenant had tacked to the wall.

❏   ❏   ❏

The massage parlor was called The Oasis. Naomi and Josie and the other girls worked 14-hour shifts. Everything smelled of sweat and incense and urine and massage oil. A lot of the time the girls just sat around, waiting for customers. This provided many occasions for smack. Josie urged Naomi to ease back, just a little, but Naomi wouldn't listen. You have to be high to even look at these creeps let alone touch them, she'd say. One evening, after they'd done up and vomited and nodded and then sat smoking cigarettes, Josie told Naomi the reason she wanted her to slow down was because she loved her. Naomi looked in her eyes and began to cry. The bell rang to go back to work. Time passed. A parade of penises and fat bodies. One Tuesday morning, Josie returned to their room from getting coffee to find Naomi lying on the floor, plastic baggy and lighter and spoon and spike scattered on the linoleum beside her.

Alphonse arrived quickly to take away the body.

Apparently God can do anything He wants, Josie realizes. She snatches up the spike and the baggy and retreats to the corner where she slumps, humming tunelessly as she watches Alphonse arrange Naomi in a body bag. And she will not go back to work at the massage parlor and more amounts of time will pass and Alphonse will return and throw her meager belongings into a paper bag and deposit it, along with her, on the sidewalk. And she will write a postcard—Dear Folks, There's been a little trouble ...—but only in her imagination, and the truth is her folks have already concluded there's been trouble, the postcards having ceased and the cosmetology schools in Denver having no record of their daughter and the police in several cities contributing nothing and the private investigator determining Josie left Denver and went to Salt Lake but after that the trail goes cold, and meanwhile the scrapbook rests on the bedside table where her mother pages through it as she softly cries.

❏ ❏ ❏

But, as we all know, one insignificant death—Naomi, in this case—cannot interrupt the designs of the heavens and they will continue their aimless revolutions, and the days and nights will press wearily and hopelessly onward, and Josie will go out and work the streets, her only option now that Zavarian has washed his fat man's hands of her. In those days, as I shuffled by on my own uncertain rounds, I must have passed her, there beneath the overpass in the day's

LYNERKIM'S DANCE AND OTHER STORIES

overbearing heat. Later in the day I might have found her still at her station in the hot night, wearing a mini skirt from Goodwill and a torn jersey slipping past a small, bruised breast, (oh, that yellow sundress), imploring the men who drive by.

But now, at this moment, weeks and months and centuries having gone by, there are few if any who will stop for what Josie has become, this creature, and so in the waning hours she will begin the long trek home. Homeless people huddle in their cardboard boxes, the last few weary hookers lean against the lamppost at the corner, in the busses rattling by the few solitary passengers slump against greasy windows, the last drunken patrons stumble from the after-hours bars and clubs with their shoulders hunched forward as if the fetid air is a storm that must be breasted, quietness of a sort coming to this section of the city called the Corridor, quietness broken now and then by a stifled cry or a gun shot or a blip of police siren. Josie has now been in the city a century, a century since she left Vegas in either the black Cadillac or the white Bentley and looked down from the mountains onto LA and beheld the carpet of stars, but now the apartment near Venus is gone, the room above the massage parlor is gone, dear Naomi is gone and her family might as well be gone because she knows she can never face them evermore. Her home now is a squat on the third floor of an abandoned building off Jackson in the Corridor. There is no electricity for cooking—the wiring has been ripped out, of course, and, regardless, the power was long ago turned off—so her diet is pretty much yogurt, pudding, bread, peanut butter, stale pizza, those things that can be scavenged from dumpsters. No plumbing either, when you need to go, you head down the hall and find a more-or-less unused corner, all this is temporary, of course, I mean, nothing this bad can last forever, can it? Josie lives in the squat with a man she ran into at a soup kitchen. He manages their money, by which I mean he takes the money Josie earns on the street and buys drugs with it. Drugs of any kind, and he knows them all from his days dealing, but his passion is heroin, loves the sight of it white and pure in a little plastic baggy, loves to tighten the rubber band around his bicep, loves the anticipation of the worm of his vein swelling blue in his arm, loves to hold the spike poised for a single delicious moment of eternity above his flesh, then loves to slide it home, the icy sharpness entering him, and last but certainly not least, he loves the rush of the drug into his blood, the rush that makes his brain grin until he falls back against the wall and slumps into quiet bliss.

So, Josie makes her way to the abandoned building where she hopes her man will be waiting with a new score he hasn't already used up. The moon rides high, laughing down at her. She climbs the rotting stairs to the third floor. Voices murmur in the dark hallways, there's a cough, a baby's cry. She pushes open the door to the squat. In the middle of the room a candle casts a pale circle of light. Her man lies just outside the light with only his sneak-ered feet and his lower legs illuminated. Josie stands at the door holding her breath. But at last the man leans forward, returns to the light. The resurrected corpse holds out its hand. In that trem-bling hand is the spike.

Long moments tick away. Only the circle of light breaks the silence.

Is Josie at last beginning to understand the great mournful secret.

She reaches for the spike.

I hand it to her.

❏   ❏   ❏

I watch as Josie wakes to the whisper of the dying moon. She scrubs at her eyes. She reaches over and gently touches my cold, naked shoulder near the eagle tattoo. (Could love's only mercy be one last solemn caress?) Rising unsteadily, we cross to the door, slip into the whispering hallway, shuffle to the stairway leading up two more stories to the building's roof.

Standing at the edge, looking out, she touches the eagle on her wrist.

The great secret, I whisper to her, is that there is no secret.

And as we fall, I know the wind she hears and feels is the same wind I feel and hear, that blue prairie wind from which there is no escape.

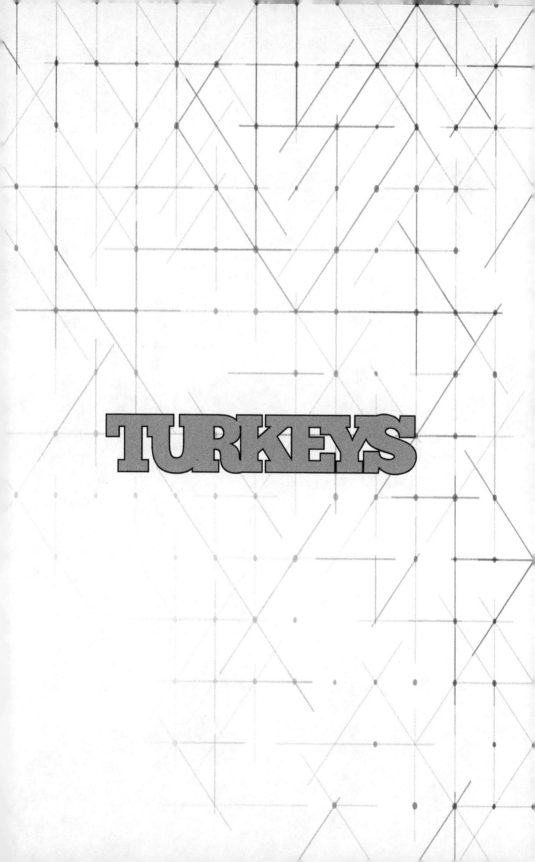

TURKEYS

I was sitting at the bar in the My-Oh-My drinking what was left of my disability check after buying oxy from the retarded janitor at the hospital. The idea of killing someone hadn't come up yet. I kept staring at the dancer in the cage in the corner. She was short and pale and had the resigned expression of someone floating in darkness just waiting for the next tragedy, exactly the kind of girl I'm always attracted to. I thought if I stared hard enough, she'd look at me, but she never did, which is typical. The retarded janitor often made strange noises and gestures, which is why they made him work in the garage where he wouldn't frighten the public. Pharmacy storage was right next door. He'd just walk over and steal pills when nobody was looking.

Various other people were drinking or shouting or passed out. I might have gone home, but they'd turned off my electric. So I just sat there getting drunk and staring at the girl and thinking about going to the bathroom for another oxy. The bartender, a muscular woman, was pouring from a bottle of Wild Turkey and for a moment I fantasized she was an angel pouring it for me because I was such a good customer, but of course she wasn't. But it made me think of the turkeys I saw driving back from the hospital.

They ran across the road in front of me, up the bank into some bushes. A big one stepped out of the brush at the top of the bank and stood there watching me. I stopped the car and stared back. It might have been the oxy I took as I left the hospital, but for

R . H . E M M E R S

some reason I knew exactly what the big one was thinking and even heard the words he was saying in my head.

So, here I am, confronted by a guy in a car. He's staring at me intensely, as if expecting me to utter some gem of wisdom that'll solve whatever inane problem he's facing. Well, here's news: I've got my own shit to deal with. The others are up in the bushes pecking at the ground for bugs to eat, especially ticks. Their thinking is simple: bugs, bugs, bugs. But, man, the stuff in my head. The thing is, you keep the flock safe from raccoons, you hide from eagles, you run away from hunters, you eat bugs. But is that all there is? Now I'm facing a situation. Scuttle away and shoo the flock to safety in the forest? Then what? Resume eating ticks and always looking over my shoulder? But a voice keeps saying do something real for a change. What the hell does that mean? What reality is available to a turkey like me? Jesus, life is baffling. Does any of it make sense? Ticks do taste good, though.

As I was getting ready to go to the bathroom this guy I hadn't seen for years came into the My. We were in high school together and we were both fuck-ups. What I remembered most about him was how he grinned all the time. It wasn't that he was trying to be funny, it was just how his face was. He got beat up a lot, of course. Hey, wipe that smile off your face! No? Bam! His name was Rod Something-or-the-Other. He looked around vaguely and then sat on the stool next to me. "Hey," he said. He was grinning and maybe it was because he was glad to see me, or maybe not. Everybody called him Smiley, I remembered. Also, Dickhead. Time passed and we got drunker. The bottles behind the bar started sparkling like Christmas lights and whispering promises. Rod muttered, "What an asshole."

"Who?"

"This guy. You don't know him."

"I wouldn't want to, if I have a choice."

"The thing is," Rod said and put his head down on the bar. For a minute, I thought he'd passed out. The bartender thought so too and looked like she was going to call a bouncer to throw him out into the alley. The alley smelled of garbage and piss; I knew this because I'd been thrown out there several times myself. But then Rod raised his head.

"It's personal," he said.

I didn't want to know anything personal. I turned away and raised my hand for another drink. The bartender ignored me.

"It was my girlfriend," Rod said after a while.

"She did something?"

"No, the guy."

"What?"

"Maybe she was drunk or high, but regardless. He fucked her."

"Wow. What did you do?"

"Nothing yet. But I should probably kill him."

❑ ❑ ❑

After they threw us out, we decided to go down to the river to this other bar we thought would let us in. It took a while to find the river—was it east or west? When we finally did find it, we rested on the bank in a little cove filled with garbage that had floated in—an old sock, bottles, condoms, syringes, a headless doll baby, the usual things. On the other side of the river, lights roared so loudly they hurt my eyes. This was a casino on a boat. It looked like the kind of place that had nice furniture, good carpets and happy people, exactly the kind of place I knew would never let me in. But Rod had the idea we should steal a boat and row across and win enough money to go to Florida where he had an aunt who managed a store at a marina.

"We could get jobs there," he explained. "We'd meet rich people and work on their boats around the world."

It was a good plan, but I pointed out we didn't know anything about working on boats. "Also, I don't think they let drunks who smell like garbage into the casino."

I don't know if Rod heard me. He was already thinking about something else. "We can't go to the casino," he said.

"I know. I just said."

"Because my girlfriend could be there."

"Does she work there or something?"

"What do you mean 'something'? Like a prostitute? Because that guy fucked her?"

"I didn't mean anything."

"You wouldn't believe the things she does." Rod looked across at the casino one last time. "She probably wouldn't be there anyway, but you never know."

❏   ❏   ❏

We left the river bank and went looking for the other bar where we could keep drinking. But when we found it, it wasn't there. There was just an abandoned building with the windows broken out and piles of rubbish. The streetlights were out and the shadows kept looking like scurrying animals that could attack us.

Rod sat down on a concrete block and started crying. He wiped snot from his nose. "This is just great," he mumbled. "We can't even drink anymore. One more defeat."

"Look," I said, "I think I see lights of a place down that way. You look." Actually, I couldn't see anything down there except more dangerous shadows.

"You can't cheer me up. But if I could kill that guy…"

❑ ❑ ❑

For a while we slept on the river bank on a muddy piece of old rug. Then Rod sat up and punched my shoulder. My first thought was that it was morning and a new day when I could make a plan I might even try to carry out. Then I opened my eyes and saw it was still night. "There's this guy we can get a gun from," Rod said happily.

The guy, Rod said, lived near Milheim, a small town down the valley. We walked back to the My-Oh-My and got my car, an old Plymouth with rusted-out fenders and an engine that burned oil and left a black cloud behind me wherever I went. My friends, those still alive anyway, would say, Here comes Smokey. Or, Here comes Asshole, if I'd recently tried to cheat them on some meth or whatever I was selling at the time. There was no other traffic on the valley highway, which was a relief because now there was something else wrong with the Plymouth and it kept wandering back and forth. If there had been traffic, it might have been an Amish family in a horse-drawn buggy with just a dim lantern on the back suddenly appearing in front of us and the wandering Plymouth would have killed them. During the day the Amish buggies were everywhere, backing up normal traffic. You always had to be alert in order to avoid the piles of horse shit they left on the road, so maybe that was why the Plymouth had decided to swerve back and forth.

"Did I know your girlfriend?" I asked as we drove along.

"She dropped out in tenth grade."

"I almost did the same thing, but my dad beat the crap out of me. This was before he died in that accident. Oh, Jesus!" I wrestled with the steering wheel to avoid something that suddenly appeared in the middle of the road. When I looked in the rearview mirror, it looked like a body wrapped up in dark cloth. It was probably just a deer, but for a second I thought, Wow, a dead Amish girl.

We were maybe a mile or two from Milheim when Rod suddenly shouted, "Hey, pull over here!"

I wrestled the Plymouth off onto some grass. It was so dark and my headlights were so weak I couldn't really see what I was doing and we crunched into a rock or a root or something and the Plymouth died. Fuck, I thought, we'll be here forever. It probably *was* a body back there and when it's light an Amish lynch mob will come after us. How'd I get hooked up with this guy anyway? No wonder they called him Dickhead when they weren't calling him Smiley.

I was about to say something that would make Rod cry again, but he was already out of the car running across the road toward a cemetery on the hillside. Its tombstones gleamed dully in the night. Most were small and square, in ragged rows like bad teeth. But toward the front was one tall one overlooking the rest. Its base was blocky and its spire looked like a lighthouse. Rod flopped to his knees in front of it. I wanted to stay in the car and dream I could change my life around. But I knew that was only a childish thought.

"See this?" Rod said when I crouched beside him. He flicked his lighter and pointed at a metal plaque on the tall tombstone with the dead person's name on it.

The whole place was creepy. There were no houses nearby, and the highway was empty, just darkness all-around. My skin felt like it was crawling. But Rod looked excited. His eyes flashed in the lighter flame as if the alcohol in him was on fire. "Supposedly, the guy buried here killed his wife. This was a long time ago. With a big knife."

"Why?" I asked.

"I dunno. Probably she was a slut too. The point is, he got off—he was some kind of big shot. Time passes and he dies and they bury him here and put up this big stone."

"Let's go find the dude with the gun so I can go to sleep."

But Rod wasn't listening. "Then, blood came out of the stone in the shape of a knife. They'd wipe it off, but it kept coming back. So finally they covered it with this plate."

"Let's go. This place is weird."

Just then, headlights appeared down the highway. We lay down behind the big tombstone. The car went by. Rod jumped up and ran across the road to the Plymouth and opened the trunk. When he came back, he was carrying a tire iron. He started prying at a corner of the metal plate.

"What the fuck?"

"I wanna see the bloody knife," Rod said. He was grunting and prying. "All my life since I heard that story, I've wanted to do this."

Well, I thought, at least he has a goal in life, even if it's a stupid one. I couldn't remember the last time I'd had a goal, probably never.

Suddenly Rod stopped. He peered into the darkness up the slope past the tombstones. "There," he whispered. "They're coming toward us."

I strained to see. At first there was nothing, just the blackness and the tarnished glimmer of the tombstones. I strained harder. "Jesus," Rod said. "It's ghosts or something." Then I saw them too. Shapes marching down the slope toward us. Whatever they were, they were making snuffling noises.

We ran back across the highway to the Plymouth. The starter ground and whined, but I finally got the engine going. "Let's go, let's go," Rod was shouting. I slammed down the gas pedal as far as it would go. The tires slipped back and forth. Then the car bounced and lurched back onto the pavement.

We were almost sideways and I hauled at the steering wheel to get us pointed in the right direction. In the process the headlights swam up across the cemetery slope. That's when we saw that the ghosts marching down to attack us were actually a flock of turkeys, a big one in the lead.

"Gobble, gobble, gobble," Rod said. He was laughing, but I knew God was trying to tell me something.

Milheim was totally dark when we got there. Nothing open, not even one of those 24-7 markets with some raghead behind the bullet-proof glass, where you could get a six-pack which I really needed. Rod was leaning toward the windshield, peering out at the darkness. "I think it's the next street," he said. "I remember there was Santa in a sleigh on the lawn right before you turn."

"Santa? It's the middle of August."

"I guess they leave it up all the time. I mean, where would you store Santa and his sleigh? It's big."

We drove another block and there on the corner was Santa Claus in a sleigh. Rod chortled happily. But as for me, I always found Santa creepy, sliding down chimneys to sneak a peek at the little boys and girls, but maybe that's just because of something that happened to me once. Anyway, I didn't say anything and made the turn. The road climbed steeply into the mountains. It was even darker here and there were trees everywhere and probably bears. "Go slow," Rod said, "so I can remember. There was a giant man with an ax at the entrance."

Does everyone here have weird things in their yard? That made me think of my father. One time when he was drunk he put a dog harness on my baby sister and tethered her to a stake in the yard. "Now, Goddamnit, carry on that wailing out here and stop bothering me!" he shouted at her. She never told me anything else he might have done to her, but I could imagine. When she was thirteen she put Drano in his coffee, just not enough. He spit it out and then went after her with his belt, worse than the last time. The next day she ran away. I never saw her again. Sometimes, I miss her; she used to listen to my idiot schemes as if they made sense.

"There!" Rod shouted and sure enough to my left was a huge man, maybe eight feet tall, holding an ax on his shoulder. I turned and we bounced down a long dirt road until the headlights found a log house. In front of the house was a Beetle up on blocks with a bumper sticker that said, "In the Event of the Rapture, This Vehicle will be Unoccupied."

"He's a very religious person," Rod explained.

"I bet he'll be a very pissed-off person if we wake him up at 3 in the morning."

Suddenly, a big, snarling dog tore around the corner, throwing slobber everywhere, but was yanked off its feet when it came to the end of its chain. The front door of the house opened and a short, fat man with a beard to his belly and hair to his shoulders came out with a shotgun.

"He never sleeps," Rod said. "At night, he sits in the dark and thinks. He'll remember me."

"What does he think about?"

"I asked him once. He said, 'You don't want to know.'"

Rod got out of the car, walked forward and mounted the porch steps. Both the fat man and the dog stared at him. The dog started snarling and slobbering again, but the fat man just kept staring. Then he smiled and put his hand on the top of Rod's head, like a priest. They went inside. The dog crawled under the porch.

About ten minutes went by, then the front door opened and Rod walked back to the car. The dog didn't even come out to snarl at him. Rod, of course, was grinning. He settled himself in the car seat, lifted his shirt and pulled out a small gun. It was tarnished and looked banged up and one of the grip pieces was missing, but it was a gun.

"Dude, you really did it," I told him. "I thought you were just full of shit."

I took another oxy. Then we drove back down the mountain to Milheim and then back past the cemetery and on down the valley to the city. I thought maybe just getting the gun would be enough for Rod and I could drop him off and then go someplace and sleep. But no, he wanted to go see the guy.

"The guy that…?"

"Yes."

Maybe it was the last pill I took, but as we were heading for the Fifth Street Bridge the Plymouth started wandering back and forth again. Eventually it got so bad we banged into the curb and bounced up onto the grass of the park that runs beside Old River Road. As soon as we came to a stop I jumped out, staggered to a lamppost and threw up. My head was spinning. The clouds seemed to be breaking apart, allowing daggers of moonlight to seek me out as if they wanted to impale me. The river was right there, not thirty feet away, with black birds as big as houses floating along on it.

Or was I just having visions? I staggered away from the lamppost. A voice near me said, "Ho, is that you, Jimmy?" It turned out the voice belonged to a homeless guy lying under a tree. But inside my spinning head, a voice was saying to me that at least Jimmy, who-ever he was, must have done something right in order to have his name called out in the night.

Eventually I managed to get back to the Plymouth and start it up. Rod was just sitting there holding the gun. We drove across the bridge to a dilapidated neighborhood of old shotgun houses the railroad built many years ago before it pulled out of the city. Now they were basically flop houses where dopers and cripples and old people with no money lived, just hoping they wouldn't get killed in one of the gunfights that often erupted.

Rod told me to stop across from a house with a porch that had fallen apart and a giant pile of old tires in its small yard. For a while we just sat there. Every so often Rod would laugh. There were sev-eral loud pops down the street—maybe a backfiring car but prob-ably a gun. Rod nodded as if a message had been conveyed.

"Well, that's interesting," he said and got out of the car.

I thought about just driving away, but finally I followed him across the street. There was faint music from upstairs, some weird foreign-sounding thing. I was still thinking about leaving but couldn't make up my mind. Rod pushed the front door open, so I had to follow.

The hallway was dim. There were doors along it, some open, some closed. Various noises seeped out: snoring, grunts and groans, an intake of breath like sucking a crack pipe, a drawn-out scream. The place smelled awful, like rotten fish and various secretions. We climbed the rickety stairs at the end of the hall. Rod went to a door behind which the strange music was playing. He had the gun stuck in his waist. He took it out and held it up. Both of us looked at his hand shaking. I thought he'd probably turn around and walk out of the building. But I willed him to stay. For some reason—probably that scream I'd heard—I felt invigorated and wanted to see what would happen.

At that moment the door opened. A young, skinny black girl stood there holding a pipe curling sweet-smelling smoke into the air. She was probably 14 or 15 and had a long, livid scar on her cheek. How sad and beautiful she looked holding that pipe! She looked like the sort of person who would wander into my dreams and come to a bad end. "I was gone down there to pee," she said. I saw a question just for me shimmering in her eyes. Then she looked at Rod and the gun he was holding. "He's in there," she said and ran out between us and down the hallway. We went into the room.

Candles burned here and there and that weird music came from a boombox in the corner. A man was lying on a mattress on the floor, his head propped against the wall. He had a beard and he looked like an old man. He was naked except for his underwear and socks. They were old-fashioned socks that came way up his legs.

Rod took a couple steps until he was about six feet from the guy. The guy didn't move at all, just stared at us with red, wet eyes that made me think he knew how demented God could be. His hands were flat on the mattress, and his fingers wiggled back and forth like little snakes, the only movement.

"Is that him?" I asked Rod.

"Probably," Rod said, but it sounded more like a question. The man on the bed frowned. Yes, I thought, he did know about God's mental state.

"Well?" I said.

Rod's hand with the gun was shaking even more. "I don't know," he said.

The dark room, the sputtering candles, the weird music from the boombox, the man lying on the bed, it all suddenly seemed famil-iar. It was like a dream I'd had, or maybe just thought I'd had, or anyway wished I'd had, perhaps one of those dreams entered by the sad and beautiful little black girl with the scar. Whatever it was, it was something real, a plan, that seemed to hover right there. Right there!

"I do," I said. "Give me the gun."

LYNERKIM'S DANCE

Never Put Off Until Tomorrow
What You Can Do Today

It was just after a tepid dawn held at bay by the apartment's thick curtains when Hickenlooper called about a new gig in Mexico.

In a circle of light cast by the Laburnum table lamp, Lynerkim was at work at his desk; this was as it had been since three in the morning— he sleeps only a few hours a night at best. This work, which has been his morning routine for many years, consists of cutting articles from the many periodicals to which he subscribes, all of them delivered to mail drops changed periodically and scattered across the city. Each clipping, with any appropriate margin notes inscribed in his scrupulous handwriting, always with a fountain pen, is then placed in a precisely labeled manila folder. GUNS. JOKES. MURDER. WILD ANIMALS. PLANE CRASHES. FEMALE VAUDEVILLE PERFORMERS. BARBERSHOP QUARTETS. SKIN DISEASES. BOY BANDS. GARDENING. THEOSOPHY. METHODS OF EXECUTION. REALITY TV SHOWS. VACATION DESTINA- TIONS. RECIPES.

And so on and so forth.

Lynerkim, on this morning (as on every morning,) worked in his bathrobe, red-and-grey striped and voluminous enough for a small tent. The fact is that Lynerkim is a very large man, easily 6-foot-6, 300 pounds, with broad shoulders, the round beginning of a belly and a huge head. That huge head is bald and gleaming, all of it gleaming, face, neck, cheeks, all of it smooth and clean and white; this is because Lynerkim has no beard, no eyebrows. In fact, his entire body is hairless. Yet, despite what might be considered the grossness of this body, the features that pattern his hairless face are surprisingly delicate: brown eyes that own an intelligent and inquisitive sharpness but which can quickly fill with tears when he reads or views something that moves him, which happens frequently; thinly compressed lips that on another man might betray flintiness and disapproval but on Lynerkim, with their slight curl at the ends, instead hint at a tick of mischievousness; a nose that is fiercely aquiline for most of its sharp length but ends in the incongruous pug of a naughty boy who just played a trick on his older sister.

Thus, hairless Squire Lynerkim.

As he worked, his radio reported the news of the day:

> "A giant asteroid first detected four years ago is on a trajectory that will bring it close to the earth this spring, but NASA scientists say there is no cause for concern. The trajectory of the mile-wide mass of hurtling rock and ice will be 'close' only in space terms: about 20,000 kilometers (12,000 miles) or, according to NASA, safely within the margin of error for a collision with earth."

He listened a moment, shook his head and kept his scissors in motion, carefully plying them around the edges of a magazine article regarding the differences between Irish step and *Sean-nos* dancing. Lynerkim, as you might have guessed, eschews much of modern electronic gadgetry, the computer in particular, even though it might aid his research; that blinking, winking box excited his fears that unnamed individuals in the government were at work prying into his life and research. However, there was one technology he was pleased to make use of, the cell phone, and in his desk was a whole drawer filled with burner cell phones, one of which now buzzed.

It was Hickenlooper, he of the softest Virginia drawl, offering a job in Mexico, in the city of La Paz to be precise. They have a man in place. The subject would be identified to Lynerkim once he was there. *They have a man in place*, Hickenlooper repeated, his drawl broadening even more.

As Hickenlooper waited patiently, Lynerkim pondered through long moments of silence. His last two forays south of the border had ended unpleasantly, each featuring difficult exits along with stomach troubles. Also, he had been looking forward to spending significant time working on his Special Project. On the other hand, Hickenlooper had always treated him well and had once helped him out of a delicate situation in Chicago involving the Russian Mafia. So, after a verbal nod of agreement, he destroyed the sim card from the burner phone, completed the clipping and filing of the article he'd been working on—"*Sean-nos dancing is similar to the more formal, competition-oriented stepdance but is more freeform in its expression*"—took a long bath, dressed, pasted on his eyebrows and hair and caught a mid-morning flight from LAX.

FILE: TSA INDIGNATIES

People Don't Take Trips, Trips Take People

Lynerkim hated flying and this flight to La Paz proved particularly hideous, filled as it was with rowdy and smelly American tourists, all talking as loudly as possible, drinking as much as they could hold, heading south to golden beach enclaves where all would be forgotten and forgiven. (Oh, the fools, he thought.) A number of travelers, passing up and down the aisle, did a double-take at the sight of the pasted-on hair and eyebrows he wore out in the world. But he was accustomed to such notoriety and could hardly blame the double-takers: He looked like a beefy Groucho as painted by Dali. But whatever. The fact was he'd come to glory in his appearance because he'd acquired a bit of secret knowledge: the more grotesque the disguise, the more unrestrained the clown can allow himself to be.

He tried to ignore his gauche fellow citizens by concentrating on the view out the window. This didn't help much.

Because what he saw, yellow bile a rising tickle in his throat, was that brutal Mexican sky pressing down upon the desert and anything that might try to exist there, and he could almost feel once more the barren wind scorching his neck and cheeks, that barren wind hurrying sand across the freshly filled graves at his feet.

He turned away from the window, he reached for his notebook and pen.

FILE: GHOSTS.

The plane fled swiftly south beneath the sneering heavens.

Within this frantically hurtling, southward-heading metal tube, there was one exception to all the laughter and manic shouting and hectic movement of the *Norte Americano* tourists. This exception, seated on the aisle two rows ahead of Lynerkim, was an older woman wearing some sort of heavy black garment, with a black scarf over her head from which wisps of gray hair escaped. Her head was bowed. Lynerkim studied her for many minutes. He worked through a number of different possibilities for her identity before finally deciding she was an elderly Mexican nun, returning to her work in the Diocese of La Paz, in the act of prayer at this moment on the plane. Prayer had always fascinated Lynerkim. Among the earliest of his files, its creation dating to his first days as a student of philosophy at the Sorbonne, is one labeled WHAT ABOUT GOD. In a sub-file labeled *Precaria* (from the Medieval Latin meaning *petition* or *prayer*) he has deposited clippings and notes on such topics as the efficacy of intercessory prayer, *Salah* as one of The Seven Pillars of Islam, apotropaic magic, the prayer to Odin in the *Volsunga Saga*, Heller's *Typology of Prayer*, glossolaia, the *do ut des* principle, Mary Baker Eddy's Fall in Lynn and the birth of Christian Science, the Cathar Pater and the Parfaits, etc. etc. etc.

A fat man in an Hawaiian shirt, carrying a dark drink in a plastic cup, stopped, stared at Lynerkim a moment, grinned, raised his drink in a toast and stumbled away. Lynerkim took no notice; he continued to contemplate. *If* she was indeed a nun and *if* she was indeed praying, what might she be praying for? An end to cruelty, this all-too-pervasive cruelty, and a blossoming of compassion in a better world? Perhaps an accommodation with this world? Forgiveness? Then what sin might a nun have committed to require God's forgiveness? Ah, the secrets we lock away, Lynerkim mused, lock away in the heart, if not soul, drawing them forth into blighted air or fearsome sunshine only when we feel the need to torment ourselves with the useless dream of redemption. If he were to pray, he thought, really pray, cutting loose the heavy straps that bound tight his heart and laying his deepest and darkest secrets at the foot of God, what would be the result? He felt his pulse beat stronger, as if he were approaching a moment of extreme danger. What if he prayed for his immortal soul to be cleansed of its many and marvelous sins?

The Fist of God would probably smash him into a million pieces, ha ha ha.

The plane circled for a landing in La Paz.

The City of Peace

Lynerkim took the bus into La Paz from the airport, accompanied by several of the tourists. They all were rowdy and they all wore shorts and, in the case of the women, skimpy tops, such attire inappropriate, in his opinion, for a country still essentially conservative in its mores, especially regarding female attire. (Speaking more broadly, the manner in which people dressed themselves was a constant irritant for Lynerkim. Not just people dressing too casually for a visit to Mexico, but people dressing too casually in general: shorts in a restaurant! flip-flops on an airplane! ball caps everywhere and not taking them off indoors!!! He always dressed smartly: coat and tie or, in an informal setting, such as on an airplane, pressed slacks and appropriate shirt, sometimes a sport coat.)

At any rate, arriving in the city he checked into a modest hotel downtown, several blocks from the bay and the main tourist area. First, of course, he acquainted himself with the hotel exits should a situation arise—an unexpected visit, for instance—requiring him to leave quickly. Then he unpacked, stowed his belongings carefully in the bureau, removed his hair and eyebrows and lay down to nap. The last thing he saw before darkness claimed his brain were the words "if you do not do what is right, sin is crouching at your door," scrolling across his closed eyes as if at the bottom of a TV screen operated by God. (Messages like this had been appearing to him in random fashion for some time now, on billboards, in banners towed by airplanes, in Jeopardy categories, etc. etc. etc.)

When he awakened, he reapplied his hair and eyebrows and descended into the delicious darkness that had overcome the lurid day.

In the hotel courtyard the fronds of the palms quivered in the breeze, sighing like bereft lovers. Birds cooed their lamentations of lost love. From somewhere deep in the city drifted a moaning wail. Lynerkim for some reason thought of the praying nun on the plane. Did she ever, he wondered, ponder God's sense of humor? What if, despite her prayers, the plane had crashed, killing all on board? Troublesome, though not all *that* humorous. Or what if the plane had crashed and only the nun had survived? Better, though not by much. But what if the plane had crashed and the nun was the *only one who died?*

He wrote in his notebook, which was always with him: GOD'S BEST JOKES.

Lynerkim set off for the bay. Clouds dissected a troubled moon. The tropic air was charged and disturbed. Heat lightning serrated the sky over the mountains west of the city. He strolled the *malecon* past new hotels with princess lights and bubbling fountains, past open-air restaurants filled with chatting patrons, some of whom would cast a glance in his direction, surprise widening their eyes before they quickly made themselves look away. When would his unknown contact make his (or her) presence known in order to point out the subject of this excursion south of the border? Was it that pedestrian he just passed on his walk who flicked a sideways glance at him? Might it have been that man wearing a greenish *guayabera* and drinking wine at an open-air restaurant called *Mariscos Azul* (not a particularly appetizing name—Blue Seafood—he thought) whose inspecting gaze did not include eyes widened in surprise and which was held a beat longer than necessary? Could it have been that American-appearing woman wearing a Red Sox cap and strolling with two teenage girls who seemed to keep her attention deliberately focused away from him? A faint unease kept tickling his nerve endings and triggering his spider sense. He did not like this extra layer of complication slathered onto the scenario. Why not just deliver to him before his flight the accustomed information package? Why this mysterious contact rigamarole? He abruptly stopped. A strolling couple coming up behind nearly collided with him. Was it possible that he was being set-up? But for what purpose?

Spider sense going crazy!

Beep beep beep.

Some meters farther along he came to an unoccupied bench upon which he gratefully took a seat, checking his pulse and trying to calm down. Stretching before him was the old yacht basin. Moonlight flickered across the water like hopping insects. There was the sound of *mariachi* music from deep in the city: sad horns, Lynerkim thought, lonely voices. Close to shore were smaller boats, but farther out a large white yacht, its decks and masts festooned with white fairy lights spilling icy glitter across the green water, lay at anchor. Lynerkim took out his small, foldable Zeiss Terra binoculars—one of several items he always carried with him, just in case—and focused them on the yacht. In the main cabin a man and a woman were dancing, moving across the cabin windows as if they were a magic lantern show, twirling, embracing, breaking apart. The man, through the binoculars, appeared to be dark-featured with a thick mane of hair and a powerful upper body. The woman, on the other hand, looked about a head shorter, slim, with blonde hair that jumped and flared as she moved. Both were extremely graceful, a trait Lynerkim much admired. He thought he might have happily watched them for hours, but presently they embraced, broke apart, disappeared. The cabin grew dim. After ten minutes they reappeared, this time descending a stairway against the side of the yacht and stepping into a rubber dinghy held steady by a crewman. A husky man in a dark running outfit followed them into the dinghy, which then churned toward shore, leaving a phosphorescent trail that sparked then faded like a dying dream.

Lynerkim folded away the binoculars, rose and stepped into the shadows of a nearby clump of palms. As he waited for the dinghy to reach the shore, a strange thing happened. In the sky, above the distant dark horizon, he beheld a blazing corona so bright it seared away the stars as if so many snowflakes had fallen into an inferno. Then, in a blink, it was gone. It felt as if his eyes, in the space of a second, had gained and lost something extraordinary that probably would never visit him again.

FILE: ALUCINARI

By this time, the dark-featured man and the blonde woman, along with the husky man in the dark outfit who Lynerkim presumed was their bodyguard, had arrived at the beach. As the dinghy motored back to the yacht, the man and the woman danced across the sand, the man humming an indistinct tune, his humming growing faster and faster until they were capering wildly across the beach, laughing, twirling and lifting their arms as if in praise to some mad god guffawing his way through the relentless heavens. They danced as if they were the only people in the world, they danced laughing as if nothing could ever touch them, as if they could go on laughing and dancing forever beneath the edge of the black sky, laughing and dancing as a falling star traced its dying path across the night.

The bodyguard watched with an expression impossible to read.

FILE: HOPELESS ROMANTICS.

Lynerkim, in the shadows, was growing bored. The dancing couple from the yacht were acting like teenagers, and Lynerkim could not abide teenagers. The only figure in the tableau he had even the mildest interest in was the husky man in the dark running outfit who stood back from the dancing couple, calm and collected, hands clasped in front of him at his waist, his eyes in constant motion, surveying the scene, ready for anything, a thoroughly admirable quality. If the man was a bodyguard, Lynerkim thought, the corollary must be that the dancing couple had to be bodies worth guarding. Celebrities? Possibly, but Lynerkim followed neither movies nor TV and wouldn't have recognized a celebrity from either of those two milieus if they jumped out and bit him on the ankle. The *written* word was what interested him, and he doubted if either member of this couple could string more than three words together into a coherent sentence. Well, that was unfair, of course; he had no idea what the couple's skills, literary or otherwise, might consist of. Probably, they were just rich—but new money, not old.

Lynerkim withdrew from his hiding place and continued his stroll up the *malecon*, leaving the couple to their capering. He nodded to people he encountered despite the odd looks he initially received. Here and there he paused to sit on a bench and gaze out at the bay sparkling in the wavering moonlight. Two street dogs, fearsome looking brutes who normally patrolled the beach scavenging for whatever food they could find and who scared the bejesus out of most people and therefore were generally kicked or pummeled with sticks when they dared venture onto the *malecon*, stopped in their tracks to regard him on his bench. They both barked at him; one, some variation of pit bull, snarled, saliva dripped from its fangs. Other people passing by took long detours into the street to avoid what appeared to be an impending attack that would tear the odd-looking *Norte Americano* to pieces. Lynerkim regarded the dogs. He nodded at them and raised the index finger of his left hand. The dogs trotted up and sat politely in front of him. He petted each in turn. They smiled at him and he smiled at them, his fake eyebrows wiggling. They trotted happily back to the beach.

Entre los Mariachis

Presently, Lynerkim rose from the bench; he'd decided to take in the old, colonial quarter of the city. This area was several blocks inland. Here he found dimly lighted streets, crumbling masonry, small shops and taverns, ancient walled homes with crosses above their doors. The air was close with the scent of ghosts and whispered secrets and guilty dreams replaying over and over. Occasionally, however, a drunk would wander by, singing loudly even as he paused to piss against a wall.

Central to the neighborhood was the *Callejon of the Mariachis,* a narrow and cobble-stoned alley glistening with music. Musicians sporting big moustaches, *caballero* uniforms and huge round hats waited here with their trumpets and violins and *vihuelas* and *guitarrons* and accordions for the call to perform at a club or private party, meanwhile offering their music to the night and the nearby smoke-filled bars. A Mexican man and woman were dancing. Then, from a bar across the street, the dark featured man and the blonde woman Lynerkim had seen earlier emerged holding hands. They too began to dance and were joined by several other couples. A woman's laugh rang out, a laugh of pure pleasure, rising from deep in her being and running in delight up the scale; Lynerkim saw that it was the blonde woman, and her laughter stirred him, strumming some inner chord he could not immediately identify, and he thought that if he could record that laugh and play it over and over through his earphones, he might eventually be able to understand what that vibrating inner chord was trying to tell him, possibly some essential truth about love and loss. But, he wondered, would it be an essential truth he really wanted to know?

He set that question aside and moved to join the dancing. (Lynerkim loved to dance but, knowing the stir he would cause at a club, rarely had the opportunity to do so except when alone at night in his apartment.) As he picked up the *mariachis'* rhythm, his odd appearance drew surprised looks, and his bulk made one woman retreat in alarm. But he danced and danced, and the *mariachis* spurred him on, and the other dancers drew back, laughing and clapping and shouting. How could such a big, strange-looking man dance so gracefully? *Que la gracia! Ai, ai, ai!* He danced and danced and danced. Here in this city. This city in Mexico. Where the air smelled of dying flowers. Where the birds called out for lost love. Where the stars fell ruinously from the sky. Where a man heard a woman's laugh and thought of death.

FILE: LOVE AND...

Lovers' Quarrel

Now, the dark-featured man and the blonde woman withdrew to the shelter of a doorway. Smiles suddenly erased, they faced each other like contestants, chests rising and falling from their exertions. Lynerkim, himself out of breath, stepped away from the musicians, waved graciously to the clapping spectators, and leaned against the dark wall of a closed shop. He regarded the faces of the lovers across the alley from him. In his opinion, lovers assume expressions of injured righteousness when they argue; they feel pride in the way they are being misunderstood. As he was considering this phenomenon, an old man in a black suit, body as thin as a skeleton, thin moustache like an old-time movie star, face ravaged into a permanent grimace, approached, leaning heavily on his cane. He stumbled into Lynerkim, begged his pardon in raspy Spanish and tip-tapped away down the alley, eventually disappearing into shadows that seemed to materialize around him.

The message which the strange old man had passed to him as he stumbled by was written on rice paper. The lettering, when he held the message to the light, was so tiny and cramped that Lynerkim puzzled over it for some moments. Then he put it in his mouth and chewed and swallowed and returned his attention to the couple in the shelter of the doorway across the alley. He watched as the man reached out for the blonde woman and as she pulled away and hurried off, her heels clicking on the rough cobbles of the alley. The bodyguard looked over at the dark-featured man, received a shrug and scurried after the blonde woman. The dark-featured man headed into the nearest bar. The bodyguard had an interesting way of walking, Lynerkim observed, his right foot hesitating before planting itself forward, as if reluctant to carry the man toward what he must face next. Lynerkim reached for his notebook before setting off.

FILE: NEUROMUSCULAR IMBALANCE

One Last Dance

Lynerkim made his way up the *malecon* again, heading away from the noisy tourist crowds around the pier and the nearby clubs and restaurants. To his left as he strolled, the bay stretched away, green where the water lapped at the base of the *malecon*, turning deep blue in the distance, out there where the horizon was swallowed by mist. Ahead of him he saw a large *palapa*, perched at the edge of the sea, its bar-restaurant sign joyfully pulsing a welcome into the night. As he drew nearer, he made out the slim figure of a woman standing behind the building on the edge of the *malecon*, facing the sea. A whisper of smoke from a cigarette rose into the humid air. Nearer still and he saw that it was the blonde woman standing there; she brought the cigarette to her lips, smoke trailed away.

The bodyguard, identifiable by his odd, lurching gait, was making for the bar's front door. He opened it; music gusted into the night; he disappeared inside.

This far from the tourist area vehicular traffic was sparse, and at the moment there were no pedestrians. The large homes on the landward side of the street were dark secrets behind high colonial walls. In his rubber-soled shoes Lynerkim moved closer to the blonde woman. From a place in the shadows he spent several long moments studying her. Her beauty had impressed him before, back at the alley of the *mariachis*; it was not the ordinary—by his standards—"sparkling" and "vivacious" beauty of, for instance, movie stars. Rather, for him, it was the beauty of planes and angles and haunting eyes that told of inner complexities and emotions set free at only the right moments. What particularly drew him—and not just from a professional perspective—was her thin, graceful neck with its perfect dimensions and curvature. How he longed to run his hand along it, feel the pliability of flesh, the sharpness of bone. He imagined the regular pulse of the carotid, the perfect tension of the anterior neck muscles and how they shaped her expressions—smile, frown, laugh, grimace.

He took in the warm scent of her that mingled with the welcome aroma of cigarette smoke—*especially* welcome since he'd quit four years ago. He took three soundless steps closer. He sniffed the air again. She flipped away her cigarette. That one small spark disappearing into the blinding night. He stood behind her. She shivered lightly. He reached to cover her mouth, at the same time bringing up his chosen instrument—the one that would send the message ordered by the note from the old man in black.

He was bent over her body, inscribing the message in blood on her forehead, when the bodyguard returned. His reluctant foot betrayed him, and Lynerkim rose at the sound.

"Nice," the bodyguard said. He was standing there with a drink in each hand. "I wondered if it was…"

This was not a time for thinking or wondering. Lynerkim took the appropriate action.

He knelt beside first the body of the woman who smelled so good, and then that of the other, and whispered the necessary benedictions.

FILE: RAZOR ACCIDENTS IN HISTORY

Birdsong

The next morning Lynerkim awoke from an erotic dream to the pale buzz of the air conditioning and a simmering ache under his lower ribs. It was, of course, the left side again. The silence and solitude of the moment here in his room were terrifyingly welcome. (There are times when he longs for the simplicity of a fatal disease, the final emptying of the body, the dissolving, the floating away, the final hoped-for disappearing.)

In the courtyard, the birds were whispering their melancholy songs.

FILE: CANCER. AVIAN COMMUNICATION.

Quantum

It has been many years since Lynerkim found the need to ponder the morality of his profession. His last excursion into the philosophy of murder occurred in Thailand on an exceedingly wet day in August of 1991 after he had completed a rather messy sanction involving a very corpulent woman, a four-foot toilet auger and a 13-inch Red Headed Centipede. After it was over and done with and he was drinking a glass of wine at a bar in Suvarnabhumi Airport prior to flying home, he was suddenly gripped by an almost overwhelming desire to place what he had just accomplished in the context of the over-arching universe that shrouds us all with its implacable logic.

Logic? Really? The more he thought about it, the more he came to realize that there was no "logic" to the universe at all. Instead, the universe must be—in fact, had to be—entirely a realm of randomness. Why? Because to believe otherwise—to assume that there was a "logic" governing all those endlessly bounding and zipping particles—would be to endow the universe with a purpose that desires a particular outcome or result. And that was a clear sophism. Who or what, for heaven's sake, would be doing the desiring? A quark? An electron, a neutrino? And what could possibly be a *desired outcome* for a quark, electron or neutrino?

In the airport lounge, he drank down his wine.

QED: The universe is random. Totally and irrevocably.

And if the universe is random, Lynerkim realized, his life and the lives of everyone who was ever born or who will ever be born are governed not by the way those lives are lived, for good or evil, but rather by total randomness, randomness in the form of a quantum roll of the dice falling out of the cosmic hand of a manically laughing God.

QED: There is no morality.

So why worry, eh?

FILE: PHYSICS AND MAGIC. DOOR #3.

An Uncertain Trajectory

While he waited outside the terminal at La Paz airport for his flight home, Lynerkim scanned that morning's English-language newspaper, which he found discarded on a bench.

> PASADENA, CA—NASA now says the approaching mile-wide asteroid, which they previously calculated would approach the Earth no closer than 12,000 miles, will actually pass by much closer: about 8,000 miles, or well inside the orbits of many satellites.

The asteroid is traveling at about 30,000 miles per hour, according to NASA. Should an asteroid of this size strike the earth at this speed, scientists say, it would have energy equivalent to that of a one-million-ton bomb, enough to wipe out most life on the planet. But scientists say there's no need to worry. The 8,000 miles by which it is estimated to miss earth is well within any margin of error.

Is God getting ready to roll the dice? Lynerkim wondered.

FILE: TV SHOWS—YOU BET YOUR LIFE

FILE: EXTINCTION.

Happily Home

Lynerkim was always happy to return home from a business trip. And if he was happy to be in his home, he was overjoyed to be in his home **ALONE**. This was because, as noted several times previously, he was, not to put too fine a point on it, an odd looking man, and although he had long ago become reconciled to this fact, he had determined to minimize as much as possible his exposure to any sort of public scrutiny and potential disdain or derision. (Of course, his professional work meant he had to risk occasional public forays. You might think—as he had himself at the beginning of his career—that his odd appearance would have been a handicap in his line of work, but he soon came to the realization that this was not true. For one thing, he quickly gained a particular competence in the art of the sanction. But also—this being another point we noted previously—his appearance acted as a sort of bizarre clown-like disguise. Surely a person so strange looking couldn't really be guilty of anything heinous; that would just be too melodramatic!)

Anyway, Lynerkim was home. He unpacked his bag and placed his soiled clothing in the laundry hamper for the girl who would come in later that week to tidy up, although there was rarely much that needed tidying, (On the days when the girl came, Lynerkim would, of course, absent himself on some business in the city, generally in some curio or antique store where they were already accustomed to him and his appearance.) After unpacking, he busied himself in the kitchen making a pot of tea, opening a small packet of *Da Hong Pao*, the most expensive tea in the world, recently sent to him by a friend and former client in Beijing. He filled his kettle with fresh water, raised its temperature until it measured 185 degrees on his thermometer, let the tea steep, poured it into a serving bowl, swirled it to mix the flavor, and then finally poured it from the bowl into his cup. It was a time-consuming process, but he took intense satisfaction in carrying it out precisely and methodically.

Teacup in hand he made his way across the room to his desk, which consisted of an antique table upon which were arranged the lamp, several files, his scissors and his Visconti fountain pen in an onyx holder. With a sigh, he seated himself and took a moment to survey the apartment, feeling for any untoward vibrations and emanations. But nothing seemed out of place.

It was a small apartment—you might have thought such a large man would install himself in a large home, but Lynerkim found value and satisfaction in a carefully arranged compactness.

Yes, a small apartment but an apartment filled with... *things*. There are Hekman filing cabinets taking up one wall of the main room. Stacked in carefully ordered piles in front of them are newspapers and magazines yet to be read, video cassettes, books, letters from correspondents here and there, all this the raw mash of his various bubbling research projects. (No computer, of course, even though it might make his work easier.) On the wall opposite the filing cabinets hang an array of tribal masks such as a Bamum bronze, a Kube double, a Baule snake and bird and many others. More precious objects and totems are arranged here and there around the room. Fourteen photographs of his dead mother, three of them showing her in her coffin. A velvet-lined antique display case containing an array of military medals, none of them his. A box of human ashes sent to him by a correspondent in Croatia. A replica of the signet ring, green agate engraved with a double triangle, worn by H. P. Blavatasky, the founder and chief theorist of Theosophy. A small bust of E. A. Poe. Several plates of reproductions from the Voynich Manuscript. A vial of dirt said to be from the graveside of Aleister Crowley. Etc. Etc. Etc. Lynerkim likes to have his things close at hand. The reason? This low, flat western city in which he lives sprawls beneath what sometimes seems a perpetually milky sky transfixed by a brass sun, a city of heat and light lacking the blurry comfort of rain, a city of big spaces and long distances, everywhere vulnerable in its absence of shadows. Whenever Lynerkim must venture into it, he adjusts his breathing, keeps his eyes in constant motion, pitches his nerves to react instantly. Thus, when he finally returns to his close, dim home, he wants only to be crowded by familiar objects, to be able to reach out and touch something that has accustomed shape. He wants no space around him—there is the danger.

His Special Research Project

Lynerkim spends a few moments reviewing the clipping-and-filing tasks next on the schedule:

VITAMINS. MOVIES. DISAPPEARANCES.

Then he sips his tea, rolls his shoulders, loosens his fingers, and is finally able to return to the special research project he's pursued for 13 years now. Hands incased in thin nitrile gloves, he places a letter squarely in front of him and carefully smoothes it.

January 8

Dear Mr. Lynerkim:

When I showed my wife your letter, she told me the event you were asking about happened so long ago that rehashing it now would serve no worthwhile purpose, just bring up a lot of old rumors and gossip. My wife is a woman who doesn't like her 'opinions' disagreed with (just ask the consistory of our church, ha ha) but I believe you to be a serious person and therefore I will make a statement, per your request.

My name is Donald R. Gotelli, 82 years of age and mind sound. I live in the town of Coudersburg, Pennsylvania wherein the events at hand transpired. You are correct in stating I was the one who found Doc Tom, as he was called in the local area.

On the morning of Dec. 5, 1969 in my capacity as an employee for the Mountain Gas Co., I entered Doc Tom's home through the basement door to read the meter, whereupon I detected an odor of smoke, sweet smelling smoke. Looking around, I came upon a pile of ashes on the concrete floor near the furnace. Said ashes were still warm. I looked all around but found nothing more. Then I looked up. Directly above the ashes was a hole in the ceiling, about one foot across. The edges of this hole were charred and blackened.

Naturally I was concerned. I went upstairs, calling out for Doc Tom but receiving no answer. Everything seemed in order, however. There was a coffee cup on the table beside the easy chair in the living room. There was a magazine over the arm of the chair. I remember thinking it was like somebody had just walked away for a minute. Next, I went into the kitchen and found everything there normal as well. Then I made my way down the hallway leading to the bedrooms. Here the odor I had smelled before was very strong to the point where I put my handkerchief over my mouth.

The bathroom door was open and when I looked in, I saw the grim sight that was the subject of your letter to me. Just stating the facts, right in front of the toilet a hole was burned through the floor directly to the basement. I detected the sweet smell of roasted meat like a barbecue. Beside the hole in the floor was a plaid bathrobe and a cane with an ivory handle such as Doc Tom made use of. On the other side of the hole was Doc Tom's pipe. Also, the lower part of a human leg all browned up and scorched. On the foot was a carpet slipper. But said slipper appeared untouched, another strange thing.

I left that house fast, as I'm sure you can imagine. Doc Tom's house was on North Main Street and I ran the three blocks to High Street to the office of Mountain Gas, where I told Mr. Levers, the assistant manager, what I had seen, and he called the police and fire.

After calming down, I returned to Doc Tom's house where a great deal of activity was taking place. Police and fire were coming and going, and people had gathered to get a look. After awhile a police officer I knew named Harry Sallade came out of the house looking sick. He lights a cigarette and says to me in words I'll never forget: "I'll be Goddamned, but it looks like old Doc Tom just burnt up!"

After that I went back to reading the meters on my route. A few days later, it was in the paper that the coroner said the cause of death was asphyxiation and burned over ninety-five percent of the body. (I have enclosed copies of several clippings I saved from that time.) Of course, the burning up of Doc Tom was a topic of conversation for many months. Everybody had their own idea. Maybe it was a short-circuit. Maybe a freak spark from the electric pole. Maybe lightning, although there wasn't any storm that day. Maybe a space comet. Anyway, one day I'm making my rounds and I run into the coroner, Dr. Moser. We pass the time of day awhile, and then I say, Well, Dr. Moser, here's something I've been meaning to ask you. What exactly was it caused Doc Tom to burn up like that?

Why, you damn fool, says Dr. Moser, that ought to be obvious. The man was a heavy smoker and he was sitting on the john taking a crap and he got out his pipe and lit it and ashes fell all over his bathrobe and burned him up! Then Dr. Moser gave me a disgusted look and went on his way.

Of course, Dr. Moser being the coroner he must be correct about Doc Tom burning up from tobacco falling on his bathrobe. But I still remember what I saw as the first person to enter that bathroom. What I saw was Doc Tom's bathrobe laying on the floor and there was not a mark on it from being set on fire or anything else. As to how that could be I leave to others like yourself to answer. I did once ask Dr. Moser when I was reading his meter if that bathrobe was still around, in the form of evidence, so to speak. He said to me, Thrown away. No need to keep so-called evidence about something we know how it happened.

That is my statement. If you should wish to write to me again, you may do so in care of my daughter and son-in-law in sunny Florida where we are going in our home on wheels.

Sincerely,
Donald R. Gotelli,
Mountain Gas Co. (ret.)

Lynerkim read the letter through several more times. Then he studied it word by word with his magnifying glass. He picked it up with his gloved hands, turned it in various directions, sniffed at the paper and the ink of the writing, studied it again with the magnifying glass looking for any hidden symbols or lettering. Finally satisfied, he returned it to its file, leaned back in his chair and contemplated the next steps.

Dental Fun and Games

Four days after returning from Mexico, Lynerkim faced a moment he dreaded: going to the dentist. His teeth were in fairly good shape—he flossed and brushed regularly, paying special attention to his gums—and he generally did not experience much pain during his dental examinations and cleaning and so forth. But he just hated having all those fingers and shiny instruments crammed into his mouth. Most of all, he hated the feeling of defenselessness occasioned by having to lie back in a chair with a bib around his neck like a child while the hygienist or the dentist hovered over him, going "ahh" or "mmm" or "interesting" or "let's look at the x-ray."

Probably, he conceded to himself, his disquiet regarding dental appointments had its origin, as do so many of our phobias, fears and loathings, in childhood. His father was generally off at his office or making his rounds, so it was his mother who took charge of such things as doctor and dentist appointments, his attire, his homework schedule, his snacks and school lunches, his allowance and so forth. The family's dentist at this time was a florid, red-faced man called Dr. Keller. He would prop Lynerkim's mouth open with a screwed device, then jam in a mirror and probe around his teeth and gums with various sharp things, talking the whole time, his breath, especially minty after lunch, spewing forth. Then Dr. Keller would go to work on Lynerkim's cavities, of which he had many. This involved stuffing other implements into his mouth, surrounding the offending tooth with cotton balls and then drilling away with one of those slow, old-fashioned drills. Lynerkim got through it by developing an inflamed hatred of the man and his minty breath, and he had to force his large hands to keep a tight grip on the arms of the chair rather than reaching up to tear Dr. Keller's moustache off. It was only later that Lynerkim learned that it was possible for a patient to receive numbing shots to cancel the pain; Dr. Keller, however, did not believe in "coddling" patients in this fashion. He drilled. And as he drilled, he hummed. And smiled.

Thirty years later, Lynerkim paid a visit to Dr. Keller, who had long since retired, grown infirm, developed kidney disease and dementia and was living in the county home. It was a short visit. Lynerkim doubted the former dentist recognized him. Nevertheless, he presented him with a scrumptious fruit basket.

He had specially prepared the fruit himself.

He peeled an orange and handed Dr. Keller several sections and then left.

The next day Dr. Keller fell into a coma after his kidneys ceased to function.

Death inevitably followed.

FILE: RETRIBUTION

The Good Hygienist

The dental hygienist, a tall black woman, got Lynerkim arranged in the chair, positioned her light and set out her tray of implements, then clipped a green paper bib around his neck. (She and the others at the office were more or less accustomed to his appearance and had either gotten over it or suppressed the urge to stare.) Lynerkim and the hygienist exchanged the usual meaningless pleasantries, and then she got to work. Clink clack scratch pry probe ouch clink scratch ouch.

Lynerkim tried to keep his mind centered on his Special Project and what the next steps would be instead of worrying about the poking and scraping. In this he was generally successful, although every so often when the hygienist really put her back into prying loose some tartar, his mental image abruptly shifted to one of a team of draft horses attempting to haul out a stump.

FILE: MEDIEVAL TORTURE DEVICES

But now, suddenly, there is a pause. A hollowness fills the small room of the hygienist, it's like the stillness before a hurricane. The light shining in Lynerkim's eyes grows brighter and brighter, growing like the blare of an oncoming asteroid. He closes his eyes, but the image of the onrushing celestial body remains as if etched into his retina.

Is this just a dream, he wonders, or is it the end?

FILE: VISIONS; RELIGIOUS ECSTACY

From the reception area at the front of the building comes a shriek. The dental hygienist's tools rattle as she drops them on her tray. She rushes out of the room. Lynerkim is on his feet. He is still wearing the green bib. The dental hygienist comes flying back into the room, all akimbo. She bounces into the equipment, blood spurts from her nose. There's a man behind her holding a gun. A young man wearing a white t-shirt and jeans, baseball cap on his head. His face is twisted into a terrible grimace. Out in the reception area someone is shouting frantically into the phone.

Lynerkim, roaring like an enraged beast, clamps a huge left hand over the young man's hand holding the gun. The hand holding the gun is tiny in his grasp. The young man is sweating and mumbling as he fights Lynerkim's grip. *You killed my uncle,* Lynerkim hears him say or perhaps doesn't hear him say or maybe dreads that he will hear him say. And then he summons all his strength and wrenches the young man's wrist, snapping it, and reaches for the hygienist's tray and thrusts a shiny scaler right into the center of the young man's left eye.

NEW FILE: VARIOUS USES FOR DENTAL INSTRUMENTS

Did the Foregoing Really Happen?

Or was it a dream/nightmare?

Searching Mr. Dante

Lynerkim, home from the dentist at last following the attendant rigamarole, rummages frantically in his copy of *Purgatorio* and finds at last the lines he'd been seeking:

> *By curse of theirs man is not so lost, that eternal love may not return, so long as hope retaineth aught of green.*

No Sleeping Pills for Him

The afternoon has unrolled. Lynerkim prepared a Moroccan carrot salad and ate at his desk as he listened to *Turandot* on the radio. There was one very strange moment when, a bite of spicy carrot poised at his mouth, he believed he heard the Princess in the opera singing about a massive asteroid approaching the earth. But that could not be! He knew the opera backwards and forwards and such a lyric did not exist! Then the moment passed.

Now it is four in the morning, sleep as elusive as usual. (But a condition not unwelcome, for over the years Lynerkim has come to value his insomnia for the pained rush of clarity it brings him, for the special feeling of time suspended. Hoping for visions, he will endure the clawing at the eyes, the hollowness in the chest.)

FILE: PHANTOMS. DELUSION.

His wig and eyebrows are heaped on the corner of the desk, which at the moment is not in its usual well-ordered condition, but instead is littered with newspaper clippings, pages torn from magazines, scraps of paper, letters, memos, photographs etc. etc. etc., all of it spilled from the accordion file that is the repository for material concerning his Special Project of these many years. On the face of the file is pasted a snatch of poetry scrawled on a slip of notebook paper:

> On Windsor Marsh, I saw the spider die
> When thrown into the bowels of fierce fire:
> There's no long struggle, no desire
> To get up on its feet and fly
> It stretches out its feet
> And dies. This is the sinner's last retreat...

Lynerkim shuffles through the rest of the spilled array—old photos, cracked and fading; a baptismal certificate; a child's report card; a copy of a divorce petition; various charts drawn on graph paper; an old, crinkled valentine card addressed to someone named Melinda—then selects a particular document.

Dear Mr. Lynerkim:

I thought this whole silly business had been laid to rest many years ago. As Coroner of Coal County, my father investigated the death in question and found the cause to be purely accidental, as you must no doubt be aware. I believe the ruling was that the deceased's robe was set afire by ashes spilled from his pipe.

Of course, in any small town like Coudersburg, there are always certain "elements" never content with the obvious truth. Following the accident, there was much wild talk, as there always is, among the *hoi polloi*. The hand of God, visitation by aliens, an asteroid, something accidentally dropped from an airplane. For a time, there were even rumors in certain quarters that the accident had a sinister aspect to it and that my father took part in a "cover up" of a criminal deed. (On one occasion, at the country club, I was compelled to physically confront an individual whom I overheard spreading such a story.)

I suppose none of this was really surprising, small towns being what they are and Doc Tom, as he was known in the community, being one of those individuals who aroused strong opinions. Some thought him a saint, others were convinced he was hiding some great sin. Adding to this was a somewhat mysterious personal history: Doc Tom first located here around 1950 or '51 but always remained close-mouthed about his life before that. He was active in community affairs, and his name was often in the local press in connection with the sort of issues that arise in a small town; about these issues he always seemed to have a position, some of which, I must confess, I agreed with. Many people saw him as a community leader and there was always talk that he should run for the borough council or even for mayor. Of course, any good will that had accrued to him was abruptly washed away when that sordid business involving a juvenile female high school student eventually became public knowledge.

But this is straying from the point upon which you wrote to me.

If the absolute truth were to be told, I must admit there were many, myself included, who were not entirely surprised to see the man come to some extraordinary and bad end. But to suggest his death was anything more than an accident—albeit an odd one—is to deal in the realm of pure fantasy.

As to my father's records, I am afraid I am unable to be of assistance. Several years after his death, all of his papers were lost in a fire that destroyed an outbuilding where they were stored.

Sincerely,
Clarence A. Moser, Jr.

Lynerkim leaned back in his chair. Usually, working on his Special Project served to relax him, allow his psyche to slip into a realm where, if he worked diligently enough, he could foresee arriving at a conclusion, even if that conclusion was that *no* conclusion was possible. (This was the sort of conundrum he relished.)

But now it wasn't working.

Idly, his mind flicking back and forth, he picked up a type-written report signed by one Wilton K. Fromeyer, who identified himself as a "doctor of geo-effects and researcher into related phenomena:"

> On the day in question, Dec. 5, 1969, after many months of increase analogous to an unconstrained fever, the SCALE of mean FLUX strength hit a PEAK of 1.3 worldwide, a condition of extreme geo-magnetic STORM which may well have seen even higher SPIKES in isolated sites such as the one in question. However, as to why any particular individual should become the FLUX conduit, as it were, may, in my view, depend on the condition of his or her surface INTEGRAL as it relates to magnetic field FLUX density.

Lynerkim read through it again. It seemed a kind of poetry.

On the day in question

> Dec. 5 1969
> analogous to an
> unconstrained
> fever
> The SCALE of
> mean FLUX
> hit a PEAK
> of
> 1.3
> worldwide

extreme
geomagnetic
Storm

This should have soothed him, but he still felt a strange sense of unease. What was it? He removed all of his clothing. Then, completely devoid of all covering, not even the pasted-on hair and eyebrows, he sat in a lotus position on the floor in a circle of moonlight, defenseless before his god.

But, of course, he understood the nature of the problem. Presently, the solution became clear.

He must return to La Paz and locate the grim old man in black who had passed him the message.

FILE: HOPELESS QUESTS

Hickenlooper Again

But the next day, before he could make arrangements to fly south again, one of the burner phones rang. "I got another call," Hickenlooper informed him, his drawl even softer than usual, his tone betraying a subtle tension. "It's complicated. Family business, so to speak. I'll put them in touch."

All Happy Families...

You may be surprised to learn that Lynerkim was once deeply in love. I say "surprised" only because based on the portrait of the man thus far presented, many of you might have inferred that Lynerkim is a totally self-contained individual whose only relationships, in part because of the oddness of his appearance, involve his work and his Special Project, and that even these are carried out at a remove, at arm's length, so to speak. That might well be true now, but it was not always so. In fact, as a child and then as a teenager, Lynerkim was quite good looking (the disease known as

Alopecia universalis did not strike him until he was in his twenties) and formed many friendships, courted girls, starred on his high school basketball and football teams (as well as with the debate team), was an exceptional scholar who all his teachers believed was destined to attend a top Ivy League university, become a Rhodes Scholar and earn a doctorate in his chosen field, then go on to a stellar career, perhaps as a scientist or an economist or even, as his guidance counselor fervently believed, as a politician—governor, senator, even higher. He collected stamps, was a Boy Scout, had a paper route. He helped the town librarian catalog books and answer inquiries. He was always prompt in doing his chores. He never talked back. He was always polite. He honored his elders.

His father, Leonard T., had been an Army medic in Germany during the War and after his discharge attended college on the GI bill and considered a medical career. His mom, Beatrice, took care of the house and cooked the meals, following Betty Crocker's book religiously, and brought Leonard a drink and his pipe when he got home at the end of the day and took care of the shopping and was a den mother when Lynerkim was in Cub Scouts and later encouraged him to earn his Eagle badge. And then something happened.

Lynerkim was in his meticulously neat bedroom one evening indulging in his newest interest: clowns. (He had finished his homework, of course.) He would search out images of clowns in newspapers and magazines, neatly clip them and paste them in a scrapbook. He would also seek out biographical information about individuals who practiced clowning, all with the serious purpose of trying to identify the reasons why people, whether amateurs or professionals, chose to disguise themselves in this manner. (The fact that his father's primary hobby at this time, was clowning—he entertained at birthday parties for young children—no doubt spurred the young man's interest.) Lynerkim's theory was elementary so far: the clown costume was a mask behind which a person could hide while allowing the escape of emotions he or she would normally keep tightly concealed, perhaps because they were unacceptable to broader society. But he was determined to refine his theory and, in particular, to address the question of why certain individuals would adopt clown disguises that appear evil. The idea of the "evil clown" wasn't new, of course—DC Comics had introduced the Joker character in 1940—but Lynerkim was determined to track down the inception of the "evil clown" trope, and his research had so far led him back to a particular incident in the 14th century called the *Bal des Ardents* (the Ball of the Burning Men) when a young French king and a number of his more frivolous retainers had dressed up as evil clowns for a masquerade ball and were set on fire by a stray flame, only the king himself narrowly escaping incineration.

There was a tentative knock on his door, almost a scraping sound, as if from an animal. Then the door swung slowly open. A face peered in. At first Lynerkim took it to be a clown face out of his nightmares; it conveyed such a sense of dread that it frightened him deeply. Then it came to him that it was the face of his father, and his fear increased. His father's face said nothing, and as he watched, his father's face slowly withdrew into the swallowing darkness of the hallway and then the bedroom door closed and this was the last time Lynerkim ever saw his father.

FILE: COULROPHOBIA

So He Blocked It from Memory

Lynerkim was eight when his father left and his brother died. Years later, he asked his mother about this. Someday you'll understand, she told him. Things happen.

What things, mom?

Oh, oh, dreadful things.

Mom?

You'll find out. I'm *afraid* you'll find out. Oh, please don't find out. I will not talk about it anymore. That man is dead to me.

Lynerkim went back to his tidy bedroom and surrounded himself with his pictures of clowns. He tried to recreate their expressions, watching himself in a hand mirror.

His father's sister, Angela, was living with them at this time. One evening he knocked on the door of her room. He entered tentatively at her invitation and found her in her over-stuffed chair reading *Peyton Place*. After a few moments, he worked up the courage to ask her what had happened to his father, her brother. She scrutinized him as he stood nervously before her. Then she said, I will address your question this one time and then no more. It was whispered in certain quarters that your father had committed the most heinous crime a grown man can commit. There was talk of an investigation. It was his decision to spare the family any further embarrassment by departing. I urged him to stay and fight but he said it was no use.

But what did he do? young Lynerkim asked.

I will speak of it no more, she said and returned to her book.

FILE: DSM-5.

Anyway...

Lynerkim has a daughter he hasn't seen or talked with for more than 20 years.

No, he was never married, but he had been in love, once, many, many years ago. She was a girl in his high school class and they dated all their senior year and then after graduation it was time to go away to college. The colleges they would attend were six states apart, and so that last night before going their divergent ways, perhaps never to be together again, their longing and fear, their hope and despair overcame them, and they made love.

Time passed and they wrote letters back and forth and they managed a visit at Christmas. One Saturday night in the spring of her freshman year a rapist broke into the apartment the girl shared with three others, who happened to be away that weekend. When he discovered she was pregnant, the intruder did not rape her. Instead, raging, he slit her throat. (There were reports of a man in a clown mask hanging around the neighborhood prior to the girl's death, but detectives were never able to identify him, let alone place him at the girl's apartment, nor were they successful in identifying any other suspects, and the case was never solved.)

As it happened, doctors were able to save the baby. Notified of their daughter's assault and death, the girl's parents rushed to the college town and there they learned for the first time of her pregnancy. They fell in love with this tiny human being who was all that still lived of their daughter and they vowed to raise her as their own and provide her with all the love and advantages they would have showered on their own dead daughter throughout her life.

Lynerkim had been ignorant of the girl's condition. (For many years afterward, he would ponder why she'd told him nothing, at last deciding she must have withheld the information for fear it would propel their relationship into some new and perhaps frightening trajectory. In this he was correct, but what he did not realize was that while the girl did indeed assume their relationship would enter some new *realm*, what she feared was that this new *realm* would be a marriage she did not desire, that indeed terrified her. For in the months during which she had been separated from Lynerkim, she had come to see both herself and her putative husband much more clearly and had realized that she had outgrown the dependent nature linking her to him for so long and preventing her from recognizing Lynerkim's self-contained nature that desired all aspects of his life to reside in their proper and *separate* places.)

FILE: YALE-BROWN OBSESSIVE COMPULSIVE SCALE

Lynerkim only learned of the girl's death several weeks after the fact when a letter from his professor reached him in Greece where he was on a study-abroad program. After some days of pondering and internal debate, he decided he should return to the States. He took a bus to the dead girl's hometown in Nebraska. He introduced himself to her parents. This was when he learned that he had a baby daughter. Eventually the parents grew accustomed to him and over the next decade or so he was able to visit his daughter on a semi-regular basis.

On the corner of his desk in his apartment stands a photograph in a simple but elegant frame he had especially made for this presentation. It is a photograph of his daughter at age14: a girl, young woman, in the photo she has just turned aside, as if to avoid the momentous click of the shutter. Her dark hair is cut short, she wears jeans and a t-shirt. On her wide-eyed face is an expression impossible to read: it's as if she's pondering a question and can't decide whether to ask it. Around her neck is a tiny dolphin on a dainty silver chain, a present from her father.

The last present he gave her.

And the next day would be the last time he saw her. This was in her grandparents' home, that one stark edifice surrounded by the endless fields of wheat. It was in the parlor. The curtains wavered in the breeze, there was a picture of Jesus on the wall. The endless fields, the wavering wind that scrapes and bleaches… Lynerkim's heart sinks in the remembrance of that moment, that moment when they approached each other, Lynerkim warily because of his new appearance, his daughter with a frowning but quizzical expression, that moment as he regarded her expression and realized that no, she was not put off by the grotesqueness that had taken possession of him during the many years past since he had last visited. No, his appearance had nothing to do with it.

It was something else.

A teenager then, she would now be in her middle thirties and would have traveled a great distance in time and space and attitude and understanding from that Nebraska of the endless fields and soul-withering wind. She's a partner in a prestigious law firm, her particular area of expertise being the defense industry, in particular those firms working on various top-secret projects involving surveillance and artificial intelligence. She lives in an expensive apartment in a glittering glass tower. She drives a top-of-the-line German car. She goes to parties and receptions and meets with clients and officials and contractors and so forth in fancy restaurants or lavish boardrooms. She lives that kind of life.

These things Lynerkim learned through his usual methods.

But what of the things he could *not* learn through his usual methods? What, for instance, was the state of her dearest heart? What about her soul in its most profound depths? Had she managed to keep in proper perspective the trappings of her life—the expensive cars, the fancy apartments, the high-class restaurants and so forth—so that her integrity remained intact and her view of the world had not skewed toward entitlement? *Of course,* he would like to know these things. Perhaps he hadn't seen her or talked with for years, too many years, but he was still her father and, despite his personal oddness and phobias, he harbored the concerns and feelings of any other father.

But there was one question above all others that he would have given everything to have answered for him.

As he sits at his desk, his gaze moves again to the photo, the photo in its special frame. Around his daughter's neck is that tiny silver dolphin on a thin chain. He feels a throbbing shiver run through his heart, hot and liquid and at the same time as cold as ice.

As he faced her in the parlor in the stark edifice surrounded by the endless fields, he saw it in her eyes.

No, it was not his appearance. It was something else.

And that is what has kept him away from her all these years.

The thought that she had guessed his most terrible secret.

FILE: ENTROPY. BROKEN HEART. GUILT.

But Work Must Go on...

So now, seated at his desk, after ending the call from Hickenlooper and destroying the burner phone's sim card and the phone itself, Lynerkim shakes away extraneous thoughts: of his daughter, of his own failures, of Hickenlooper's strange call. And thus he is able to refocus and so takes up a letter of the most florid penmanship, purple ink on pink paper with a cascade of roses at the top:

> ...despite the nasty media sensationalism surrounding the court action brought by my parents against his estate, he will always abide in my heart and thoughts. Certainly, the fact that I was 15 years old at the time while he was over 60 provided ample fodder for those determined to see scandal in any sort of love they could not understand or imagine for themselves. But I remember him as one of the kindest, most charming, interesting and considerate men I've ever known. And, of course, one of the most troubled, though he tried his best to hide his self-tortures from me.
>
> As one ages—and I am 67 now—one's memory often acquires a merciful haziness regarding matters that were so troubling in the past. But even after the passage of more than 50 years, my remembrances of my all-too-brief time with Thomas (though everyone called him Doc Tom, he was always Thomas to me) remain crystal clear. We were in love. We were going to marry as soon as I was of legal age. We snatched whatever brief time we could,

between Thomas's practice and my school, to be together. How happy we could be, just sitting together, talking, holding hands. And, of course, the rest of what love is all about. (As inexperienced as I was, how joyful it was.)

But it was also clear that Thomas was an extremely troubled man. Over the months before his death he seemed to be struggling to deal with some great difficulty or to come to terms with it. Why this was occurring when it did, I had no way of knowing at the time.

At any rate, when I would ask him about how he was feeling, he would always find a way to deflect my concern. But it was apparent his struggle was growing more intense day by day. He was losing weight. Sometimes, he would stop in the middle of a conversation and stare straight ahead, his eyes bright and feverish. I don't know how to explain it; it was as if he was seeing a vision or hearing a distant voice. Eventually, he would return from wherever he'd gone and make a joke about it.

It grew worse, especially during the final weeks. I know this will sound like an Edgar Allan Poe story, but it was as if something was pursuing him. His quick movements often seemed somehow defensive, if that makes sense. There was the staring, as if he saw an assailant in the distance. I could feel fear emanating from him. I suggested several times that he should go to one of the other doctors for a check-up. He would thank me and say he'd think about it. The last night, I managed to sneak over to his house after telling my parents I was going to meet another girl at the library to work on a term paper. Thomas was lying on the sofa. He seemed asleep. I said his name and touched his shoulder. He slowly opened his eyes and looked at me with the bleak expression of someone who sees no way out.

"I've been trying to pray," he whispered.

I said something rather commonplace about the benefits of prayer I'd heard in Sunday School.

"There are some sins that can never be redeemed," he replied. This will sound terrible because of the end that came to him, but it was as if a spark had entered him and he was only waiting for it to flare.

We sat in silence for some time, not touching, and then he made me leave by telling me he needed to sleep. The next day I was in class when the news came about the terrible thing that had happened. I broke down and had to be taken home by my parents. I was so distraught—nearly hysterical—that I ended up telling them everything. They shipped me off to a boarding school in California so I missed the funeral, the local furor and my parents' lawsuit.

There is only one thing I might add. It took me many years—and many hours of therapy— to recover, but finally I was able to take a more or less dispassionate view of what had happened. About ten or fifteen years ago, still curious about what might have been at the root of Thomas's troubles, I managed to locate his younger sister, Angela, then living in a retirement community in California. (Initially, I tried to locate Thomas's wife but learned she had died some years before.) Angela had lived with Thomas and his wife and their two sons for many years—this was in Thomas's former life, of course—and it was my hope she could clear up at least some of the mystery. I contacted her by phone. Eventually, I asked my question. There was a long silence. Finally, in an anguished voice, she said, "The horrible, horrible things they said he did … The rumors, the gossip… Lies, lies… But the police mishandled… They… No, I just don't know."

Then she abruptly hung up.

Lynerkim picks up the letter, he views it from several different angles. He tastes it with his tongue, he smells it, he runs his fingers over the letters like a blind person reading Braille.

FILE: BIBLIOSMIA

He Had an Intuition

The call Hickenlooper had promised finally comes on a Tuesday morning, a burner phone buzzing in the desk drawer like a ravaging insect. Sickly light bleeding around the drapes, Lynerkim standing before his desk in flowing caftan, drinking tea. The sickly light presaging the day's sickly yellow heat. The phone buzzing. In the coming days he will often remember how he'd debated answering it.

Can a thing exist without being perceived?

If the telegram is unread, does the victim still live?

The buzzing persists, insists, conquers.

"Do you recognize my voice, old friend?"

Phone to his ear, Lynerkim parts the curtains a fraction to scan the street even though he knows he will see nothing but the hammer of the coming sun and heat.

"Your silence tells me you do," the phone insists. There is an exhalation of breath like a dying sigh. "I'm just calling to invite you to a party. Jerry's place. Cocktails at 7."

Relaxing at the Lake

Lynerkim, fake hair topped by a wide-brimmed straw hat against the sun, waits on a shaded bench near the statue of General MacArthur. The park's lake shimmers before him. Heat lightning flickers against the eastern sky. The scorching breeze from the desert brings the smell of smoke. The sky is white and dead. He is whistling an aria from *Tosca*.

"It's been awhile. I wasn't sure you'd remember Jerry's place." A man in an Hawaiian shirt and cargo shorts, Braves cap pulled low, newspaper in hand, has slipped through MacArthur's shadow to take a seat on the bench.

Pushcarts clatter by on the walkway selling *churros* or *kim chee* or hotdogs with mayonnaise. There are families with baby carriages. Children run and shout. In front of them an orange juice vendor squeezes juice for a boy who looks Korean and two teenage girls wearing *hijabs* over their jeans. A boy with a yarmulke pinned to his head waits in line. Out on the lake two Mexican boys in a canoe are splashing each other with their paddles and laughing like maniacs.

"That right there, that's America." The man in the Braves cap nods toward the scene in front of them, at the juice cart, sets his newspaper on the bench beside him. "All races, all religions mingling happily." He lights a cigarette. "Oh, yes, everything is just swell... until they start killing each other like they do in the rest of the world. That dumb asshole we have in the White House, that's the one thing he got right. Keep them all out, huh?"

Lynerkim scratches the left false eyebrow where he didn't quite get the glue correct. "They should have life jackets," he said suddenly.

"Huh? The *A-rabs* should have life jackets?"

Lynerkim gestures toward the boys in the canoe, who are now rocking it violently back and forth, their laughing growing more and more uproarious.

"Anyway, cocktails at 7 minus 6 would be 1 p.m. and so here you are," the man in the Braves cap says. "And so here we are."

"A very hot one today."

They sit silently for some moments, contemplating their sur-roundings. Finally, the man in the Braves cap scratches his belly and says, "It's a special job. National security, blah, blah, blah."

Lynerkim's vision shifts to the eastern mountains where light-ning blossoms like flares over a distant battlefield. Suddenly, even though he sits on a bench in the middle of a park in the middle of a large city in this year of our Lord, he can hear the thrashing of heli-copters, the hollow thunk of mortars, the spitting of M-16 rounds. The sounds of battle mount until they're nearly unbearable. Then, abruptly, they end. He shakes his head as if clearing it. "The G and I never did get along too well," he says after a moment. "Besides, unless things have changed in the last two years, the Council has its own people."

"But temporarily without assets in place, and this job has some time sensitivity. An auditor for a defense contractor is preparing a whistleblower complaint, and has retained counsel, a lady lawyer. This contractor is engaged in very important facial recognition and surveillance work and the Council wants to see it proceed to fulfillment. Now, as to the complaint itself, it..."

"Oh, no." Lynerkim starts to rise. "Someone help!" Out on the lake, the Mexican boys have capsized their canoe.

The man with the Braves cap has disappeared as if he might have been just an apparition in the first place, only his newspaper folded on the bench evidence of his existence.

FILE: METHODS TO RECOVER FROM DROWNING.

Mozart

Lynerkim returned to his apartment and set the newspaper on his desk. He felt a strange, sudden reluctance to open it, even to touch it. So he went to the kitchen and engaged in the calming ritual of making tea. Back at his desk, he forced himself to unfold the newspaper and from its pages withdraw a small, sealed envelope. He added the newspaper itself to the stack of periodicals to be examined and clipped at some future date and placed the small envelope squarely in the center of his desktop, adjusting its placement several times until he was satisfied that it was exactly centered. Still feeling that strange unwillingness to begin, he turned on the radio. It was already tuned to his favorite classical music station but instead of music what he thought he heard—but perhaps didn't—was:

> "...maybe only 2,000 miles, but they emphasized there is no danger of it actually striking our planet."

Then the second movement of the *Jupiter Symphony* began, with those opening phrases Lynerkim always found so haunting. But now they failed to entice him; instead he twisted rapidly up and down the radio dial searching for more news. But every news channel provided only static.

He hurried to the window and parted the curtains. He scanned the sky. The brazen sun smashed against the glass pane like a hammer, its sound a great booming across the sky. Lynerkim clapped his hands to his ears as a child might. He examined the sky with the despairing intensity of a man searching the hopeless desert for the scent of water or perhaps the same man scavenging his own hopeless heart for the long-missing aroma of God.

Then, with a roaring rush like the exit of a million bats from a dark cave, the sound emptied from the heavens leaving behind a void deafening in its terrible silence.

Coffee Break

Hickenlooper left the Starbucks, *caffe misto* in hand, surveyed the long mall corridor crowded with shoppers, mostly women, and found a seat at a plastic table near a stairwell in front of the GAP that could be the GAP in any mall in America. He laid his newspaper on the table. Presently, a man wearing cargo shorts and an Hawaiian shirt, Atlanta Braves cap pulled low, wandered by, paused and turned toward Hickenlooper with hand raised in greeting as if accidentally coming upon an acquaintance. Hickenlooper nodded and the man took a seat across from him.

There were a few moments of contrived small talk—just in case they were overheard by passersby or, more critically, picked up by some listening device—then the man with the Braves cap smiled, did a little three finger quadrille on the tabletop and said, "We should start with a status report, no? Regarding the latest sales effort?"

Anonymous white light fell from the mall ceiling, anonymous shoppers pattered by looking into the windows of shops that were replicas of the windows of shops in a thousand other malls; an aroma consisting of equal parts air freshener, warm electronics, cinnamon bun and hospital antiseptics wafted through the anonymous air, tickling Hickenlooper's sinuses and pushing them toward the edge of a sneeze. Places like this always depressed him and reinforced his sense of being out of place, which is no doubt why the man in the Braves hat selected it—anything for an advantage, even if one wasn't needed.

Hickenlooper stared at the other man for a moment. "A status report?" he said finally. "I'm not really sure what I could report. I thought my role was... 'arranging' I suppose is the correct term." He ventured a smile. "The rest was then your baby and my uh, role, was uh, done, completed, as it were."

The man in the Braves cap made no reply. His face was impassive; an absolute stillness came over him. Hickenlooper, who generally maintained an optimistic view of life and held his fellow man in high regard unless circumstances pointed otherwise, felt a sudden chill, as if he had brushed up against something cold. Involuntarily, he sat back; any smile left in his system drained away.

Moments pass. There is shouted laughter from somewhere up the long mall corridor. Shoppers flit by, bags full of purchases fluttering. Hickenlooper feels a change in the atmosphere; it's as if all these passing shoppers are consuming all the air—all of it!—leaving him nothing. Beads of sweat on his forehead, beads of sweat trickling down his back.

"I don't understand," he finally manages to say.

The man in the Braves cap taps the tabletop again. "It's your man. Your job will be to put him in the right place at the right time."

"My man? You mean..?

"Yes, indeed," the man in the Braves cap interrupts, raising a finger to caution against the uttering of names.

"But, why? I mean…"

"Do you really want to ask why?"

"Uh, yes."

A pause. Then a smile, at last, but a chilly one. "That little fiasco south of the border."

"Fiasco? I don't understand."

"Yes, you do. And now the stars have aligned."

"What?"

"Let's go get some ice cream."

Ready, Set… No Wait a Minute

If he had been reluctant simply to open the newspaper, it was with even greater unease, even a species of apprehension, that Lynerkim contemplated the briefing sheet for the assignment handed him in the park by the man in the Braves cap.

This was a novel feeling for him. It was not that there hadn't been past assignments which, in the planning stages, had caused him worry, but those anxieties had involved the *methods* which carrying out a particular sanction would require and had passed quickly enough once he had successfully stalked the lion of the solution across the veldt and everything had been worked out satisfactorily in his mind: the lion in his sights and a clean kill being the certain result. And certainly there had been those assignments during which something—a sudden unlooked for appearance by a child at the bedroom door, a blind nephew knocking over a stack of books in an adjacent room and causing the subject to look up at just the wrong moment, a Mastiff watchdog fighting off the effects of the drug just long enough to offer a weak but alerting bark—something untoward had occurred to warp the declination of planned events several degrees out of whack. But Lynerkim was always prepared for events to intrude upon his careful preparations and knew how to improvise. (Granted that sometimes the improvisation could reach heights of absurdity. Once, infuriatingly stymied by a diversion that failed to divert, he'd found himself thundering up a stairway singing the *Nessun Dorma* from *Turandot*, his favorite opera, at the top of his lungs to fall upon and dispatch the befuddled bodyguard of a bed-ridden former Bosnian Serb commander who had ordered various outrages against defenseless civilians and was the target of the sanction. The sanction was successful, by the way.)

But this assignment? Lynerkim does not understand the disquiet he feels about it. After all, it seems straightforward enough—follow the whistleblower, choose a location, kill him.

He sits back in his chair, working to dispel the effects of that latest roaring asteroid episode that had abused him. He recognizes that such episodes seem to be arriving more frequently of late, these assaults on his composure: something to do with the current state of the atmosphere, he assumes, and the episodes will cease when all returns to equilibrium. Therefore, he must just put up with them for the moment.

With the help of the *Jupiter*, which he has found again, and several deep breaths, he works his thoughts back to the current assignment. Could it only be paranoia, what he's feeling? Perhaps, although he's intelligent enough to understand that paranoia, if kept within reasonable bounds, can have its uses. (And that there's a fine line between paranoia and reasonable suspicion.) But no, the more he thinks through the current situation and his feelings regarding it, the more a particular image keeps flashing into his brain. It is there for just a fraction of a second and then gone, only to return at some subsequent, unlooked-for moment. Black and white, not entirely distinct, wavering like a pirate treasure, or a disintegrating wreck, or a dead body, under water. The dark interior of a run-down café off a side street in Marseilles. There are hunched, shadowy drinkers scattered here and there, old pop tunes on the speaker system, a brief flare of light as the door opens, then closes again. He is sitting at a table to the side nursing a glass of wine, waiting. False hair in place, moon face overhung by the bill of a cap. It has to be at least twenty years ago; his features must retain some hint of youth, although the murkiness of the vision makes it difficult to tell. Another flare of light from the door, the one he is waiting for enters, peers around through the murk and cigarette smoke, sits opposite him, orders coffee. The man from MacArthur Park, but no Braves cap this time: an appropriately younger version of the man who left behind on the bench his newspaper and the briefing paper disguised in its folds.

The man begins to speak. "The Council is disappointed..." he says and that is the end of the vision. It will repeat and repeat, the vision, this mental shard, this wavering mental shard, but with nothing more than that. Nothing more definite than that.

Lynerkim concentrates. He tries to bring it clearer. He tries to separate it from the clangor that occasionally assails him. But he fails.

So, he isn't even sure that meeting in Marseilles actually took place. When the vision comes and then goes, all that is left behind is the feeling of shadows and ghosts.

Paranoia or reasonable suspicion? Does it really matter?

Because what he cannot escape is the feeling that the real target of this assignment is not the whistleblower.

FILE: DYSCRASIA

Hickenlooper Takes a Walk

Hickenlooper is strolling his favorite woodland path. All around him the soothing flutter of leaves, the soft flex of branches; in the distance just beyond the trees, the calm spread of a green meadow lifting gently toward low hills.

He needs this time in nature to think, to consider his options, plan his moves, run the scenarios: too many strange whispers have reached him lately, strange and dangerous, marring his sleep, leading to sharpness with his wife, propelling his natural paranoia, heightening his spider sense.

He turns aside to a narrow rock-shrouded outlook above a swift stream. Here after several moments he is joined by a young man wearing a blue sweatshirt and gray jogging pants.

Hickenlooper waits for the young man's breathing to slow, then says: "I need you for a special job."

The young man's only acknowledgement is a lifted eyebrow.

"A protection job," Hickenlooper tells him. "The usual rates and so forth. Should be fairly straight-forward…"

The young man regards him. There is a shadow in his eyes, a disquiet, a suspicion, an unrest, a look that Hickenlooper can't precisely define but understands all too well… because of what he is feeling himself.

"As usual, tactics are up to you," he explains. "All very straight-forward," he repeats and as he says it, he understands how lame that sounds.

The young man's gaze remains steady. "As *usual*? But this is not the *usual* way we *usually* do business. We do not *usually* meet like this. So, what is it you aren't telling me?"

Hickenlooper reflexively pats his pants pocket but, of course, the pipe and tobacco are not there: his new rule is that they don't accompany him on these walks in the woods. (But this would be the perfect time for all the fiddling that loading a pipe and getting it lighted properly entails, all that deflection, wouldn't it?)

"What I'm not telling you," he finally forces himself to say, "is what I don't know myself. This involves one of my contractors, and it's just that... It's just that something doesn't seem right. There's a feeling. I wake up at night and there's a feeling." He shrugs and wishes again for his pipe, wishes this young man were just some anonymous creature he could send into combat like a lifeless plastic chess piece instead of a flesh-and-blood human he has come to like and value over the past three years of assignments.

The young man turns in the direction of a bird song, holds the pose a moment too long, turns back. As Hickenlooper watches, the man seems to withdraw into himself, a sort of gathering of his faculties, a kind of stiffening. Hickenlooper is accustomed to this, this man's method of contemplation, his form of meditation, and waits patiently.

Until at last the young man shivers and smiles a brief smile and brushes back his dark hair and nods and says, "Ok."

"Good enough." Hickenlooper starts to turn away toward the main pathway.

But the young man stops him briefly with a hand on his shoulder. "But maybe it's you," he says. "Maybe it's you who needs the guarding."

"Me?"

The young man only smiles, a sad wan smile.

Hickenlooper nods. "Yes," he says. "Yes, you could be right."

An Accounting: Memory Renewed

Dear Mr. Lynerkim:

Please find enclosed my report regarding the matter for which you hired me. I believe that this report provides as complete a picture as possible regarding the activities of the individual in question up to and including his strange death. (Also enclosed is an invoice and an accounting of my hours spent on this investigation, along with my expenditures for travel, lodging and incidentals.)

As you'll see from the report, arriving at a complete and final explanation regarding the causes of the fatal 1969 incident is impossible at this late date. Over the course of the three days spent in Coudersburg, it became clear that none of the evidence compiled by the authorities or others has survived. (I have included depositions from several individuals with knowledge of both the incident and the subject individual, and as you'll see they add few details if any to the information you had obtained before you hired me.) In regard to any evidence, even if it did still exist, I doubt it would be helpful inasmuch as scientific investigation of the few similar incidents over the last 100 years has failed to arrive at any definite explanations. (Your own research into the phenomenon will certainly have shown this to be the case.)

Even though I was unable to provide a definitive answer in regard to what caused the incident, it was possible, as you'll see from my report, to develop fairly complete background on your father from the time he left your family, following the death of your brother, up to his own death in the Coudersburg incident. I want to warn you that the details of the horrific June, 1954 incident during which he *allegedly* was responsible for the death of your brother will be difficult to read and might dredge up extremely painful memories for you since you were the one who discovered your brother's body. As my report points out, the police were never able to conclude whether the death was accidental or otherwise (that it was perhaps due to a manic episode or something similar) and eventually ended their investigation given that by that time your father had disappeared completely. One fact that is probably not significant but which I will pass on to you for what it's worth: your father's death in Coudersburg occurred exactly 15 years after the fatal incident which resulted in his leaving your family.

If I can be of any further service, please don't hesitate to contact me.

Sincerely,
James V. Grimaldi
Private Investigator
Lic. #456397

Lynerkim's lips twist into a grimace. He runs a finger over the green agate of the Blavatasky ring, wishing for its incoherent powers, he stares at the Bamum bronze mask on the wall with its weird expression of deadly laughter, with its giant ears, its headdress of curling and hissing snakes. He rises and moves to the window, parts the curtains a fraction, surveys the street for enemies who might be stalking him, raises his eyes to the heavens wondering if the object is there that might obliterate the planet.

He returns to his desk. Studies the investigator's document again.

The report might "dredge" up painful memories?!? Good God! You mean the memories that he blocked out for so long, the memories of his brother's mutilated body, and the memories that recall the look on his father's face

The grimace. The grimace that slowly gives way to a smile.

Oh, the terror of that smile!

A SMILE…

A Smile…

A smile…

a smile…

smile…

But what he does not know, and probably will never know, is what his brother saw.

What his brother saw that required his death and thus set all these horrible things in motion.

FILE: AUTOBIOGRAPHICAL MEMORIES
AND THE HIPPOCAMPUS

Another Uncertain Trajectory

Lynerkim had received supplemental orders from the man he'd met at MacArthur Park, transmitted to him by Hickenlooper. (Strange orders. He'd tried to contact Hickenlooper for a clarification, but his calls went unanswered.) So, in his carefully restored and pains-takingly cared-for Jaguar XK120, he drove to the western environs of the city and parked in the camouflage of a line of Mimosa trees looking out on a park near the ocean. The marine layer was swiftly spreading inland, the sky darkening, the air growing chilly; in the freshening breeze the petals of the mimosa trees swirled like purple snow. From this position he had a clear view of the leafy parkland that extended from the campus of the defense contractor whose auditor was preparing a whistleblower complaint.

Lynerkim studied the scene with his Zeiss Terra binoculars. As he was beginning his second sweep, an authoritative voice on the radio gravely intoned: "NASA is now sending mixed signals regarding the closeness of the asteroid's passage…"

When Lynerkim looked down, he realized the radio was turned off.

But the voice continued with more warnings.

Then it abruptly disappeared.

The reluctance he had felt regarding this assignment, the misgiv-ings that he could never quite identify, remained with him. They rippled through him as he moved his binoculars from the contrac-tor's campus across the parkland and then back, but their mean-ing, if any, remained remote, like a distant sound from a dark for-est, a rustling, a snap of twigs, a low growl.

But it was time to get on with things.

The park seemed a peaceful place: no chattering masses, no push-cart hawkers crying out their wares, no statues, no lakes in which Mexican boys might drown; instead, it was a place of quiet trees and even quieter meadows, pathways covered with bark winding through green groves, here and there the chirping of birds and the skittering of squirrels, occasional glimpses of shy foxes. But this apparent peacefulness, of course, aroused all of Lynerkim's danger antennae, honed to purposeful sharpness over all his many years of staying alive during the practice of a profession in which death could assail him at any moment.

Presently, a man appeared at the park's entrance adjacent to the campus of glass buildings. He was a short, fat man wearing a puffy jacket and a Tyrolean-style hat with a feather, around his neck binoculars and in his hands a small notebook. He clearly matched the photo of the whistle-blower. He strolled into the park along a bark path, occasionally, as Lynerkim watched, pausing, cocking his head to the side as if listening, then bringing up his binoculars to gaze into a nearby tree. He would hold this posture for some moments, then lower the binoculars, a broad smile arching across his chubby face. He would take out a ballpoint pen and write in the notebook he was carrying, then resume his stroll.

Lynerkim felt his unease tick up another notch. Although his professional pride had meant he could not, in the end, turn down the assignment he'd received that day in MacArthur Park, his natural sympathies lay with whistle blowers of any stripe: their acts took courage and provided a public benefit he knew he could never hope to match. And now to learn that this particular whistleblower, whose demise he had come here to accomplish, was also a bird watcher! Bird watching was a hobby that had long fascinated Lynerkim although he'd never had an opportunity to take it up, his other interests always intruding. It somehow didn't seem right to kill a short, fat bird watcher, who was also a short fat whistleblower.

But he also had the sense that the real source of his distress lay somewhere else. He just couldn't bring it to the surface. There was something residing there. Something... Something... dark. His father? His daughter? The man in the Marseilles café?

SOMETHING...

Something...

something…

something…

something…

For some inexplicable reason he kept hearing the voice of the announcer from the radio that was turned off.

"Scientists say there is still no danger that the asteroid will strike the earth…"

buzz crackle buzz whizz szzzzz…

"But they note that while it is 100 percent certain the earth will be hit by a devastating asteroid at some point, it is not 100 percent certain this asteroid…

Buzzbuzzbuzz

"…just days after coming back from a shutdown due to an earthquake, Arecibo captured images of the asteroid and determined it is at least 1,465 meters across and at least 300 meters wide. If such a body impacted…"

"…life on earth would be…"

buzz crackle buzz whizz szzzzz…

But despite all the weirdness going on in his head, he managed to keep his focus on the strolling bird watcher.

Meanwhile:

> *A long, dark BMW pulled to the curb some fifty feet behind Lynerkim's Jaguar.*

An older woman wearing a dark windbreaker and jeans came down the sidewalk with a puffy-haired dog on a leash trotting beside her.

A city bus rumbled by and stopped a hundred feet farther on. No one got off. No one got on. The bus sat there, motor churning.

A male jogger ran by. He wore a blue sweatshirt and baggy gray sweat pants with a knit cap on his head. He nodded at the woman walking her dog as they passed each other.

A door on the passenger side of the dark BMW opened, then closed without anyone getting out.

As Lynerkim watched through his binoculars, the fat little man, the bird watcher, paused, took off his Tyrolean hat, put it back on again. He wrote something in his notebook, then he strolled on, heading toward the distant tree line. Lynerkim had the impression he was deliberately trying to appear casual.

The male jogger in the blue sweatshirt returned from the other direction. He stood near the rear of the dark BMW, hands on his hips, bent over slightly, breathing deeply. On the other side of the park a woman emerged from a pathway through the trees. Lynerkim focused his binoculars. She wore a scarf over her short, dark hair. Dark glasses hid her eyes. She carried a briefcase in her left hand. A dark brown purse was slung over her right shoulder. She lifted her dark glasses and looked in the direction of the fat little man, the bird watching whistleblower. He returned her gaze, and after a moment they walked toward each other.

The whistleblower and now, his attorney.

They stood close together, their heads bowed slightly toward each other. From their expressions, enlarged by the binoculars, it appeared to be a serious conversation. Lynerkim lowered the glasses and sat back to consider his course of action. Idly, he regarded himself in the rearview mirror, prodding at the thick, pasty flesh of his face, adjusting his wig and false eyebrows. *Who are you? Who? Who? Who? Who?* he hummed.

Then, as he gazed into the rearview mirror, he caught movement in the BMW parked behind him: a shadow darker than the dark interior of the car passing behind the windshield. The passenger door opened. A man wearing an olive shirt, jeans and gloves stepped out; his face was covered with a ski mask patterned like the face of a grimacing clown with a slashing blue mouth and bright orange nose. Pulling a pistol from behind his back, he ran forward toward the passenger window of Lynerkim's car.

Before he could fire, the jogger in the blue sweatshirt who'd been standing by the rear of the BMW tackled him. They went down hard on the asphalt sidewalk. The jogger knocked away the pistol and, riding on the back of the man with the clown mask, fought for the hold that would break the gunman's neck.

His topcoat flaring, Lynerkim flung open the door of the Jaguar and hustled around to the struggling men, surprisingly nimble for such a big man. The breeze rose and tore away the broad-brimmed hat he wore to hide his features when he was out. He saw the whistle blower and his attorney look over curiously at the struggling men and start walking toward the scene. "Jesus," the man in the clown mask said, and the jogger broke his neck with a crack, then sat back on his knees, breathing heavily.

He looked up at Lynerkim. "Hickenlooper… sent me…"

"Hickenlooper?"

"To protect you."

"Protect *me*? From what?"

"From…" the jogger started to say. But before any more words could emerge, blood gushed around the knife protruding from his mouth, and he toppled forward, and he was dead. The older woman wearing the dark windbreaker and jeans, but minus the puffy-haired dog, looked down at the jogger and reached to retrieve her knife.

Lynerkim grabbed her, bent her over his knee and broke her back. That was when, out of the corner of his eye, he saw a skeleton-thin old man in a black suit stumbling toward him. He had a thin moustache like an old-time movie star and a pock-marked face ravaged into a perpetual grimace. He had descended from the strange, parked bus. He tossed away the scabbard of his cane and kept coming with the cane's sword outstretched.

Lynerkim sought frantically for the pistol the jogger had wrenched away from the man in the clown mask. A great and sudden light blasted from the sky like a roaring comet. He saw the pistol lying in the grass.

The old man in black was nearly on him. He was shouting at Lynerkim: "You killed the wrong one! You killed my daughter!"

Lynerkim recognized the old man who had passed him the note in La Paz. He had the gun in his hand and shot him three times in the chest.

He sensed movement to his right. He turned and fired again.

The woman who had been talking with the whistleblower toppled to the ground and lay there twitching. Her chest was covered by blood. Her briefcase lay beside her; the dark brown purse and dark glasses were discarded some distance away. Lynerkim saw the whistle-blower running away into the trees on the other side of the park.

The woman twitched and then was still.

Knees cracking, Lynerkim bent down beside her. And that was when he saw, or thought he saw, the emblem dangling from a dainty silver chain around her neck.

A Final Entry in the File

It is scrawled in pencil on a piece of roughly torn tablet paper. Written in extreme haste, many of the words are barely legible. As if an irreconcilable deadline had been pending.

THEORIES TO EXPLAIN THE PHENOMENON

1. Household factors, e.g. careless smoking, trapped gas from heater, dropped match, malfunction of equipment, etc. etc.
2. Geomagnetic flux. Buildup of earth magnetic forces at particular time/place creating optimal conditions for Spontaneous Human Combustion.
3. Malfunction in digestive system whereby energy from complex processes in stomach creates excess of heat, thus igniting fatty tissue.
4. Electrical fields. Overhead electrical lines, electricity transferred to human body creating enormous static charges leading to SHC.
5. God.
6. Terrible sin

The paper rustles in the starlit breeze from the open balcony doors.

The Solution to Everything

Straddling the railing of his balcony, four stories above the concrete pavement, his voluminous red and gray robe flowing in the starlit breeze as if flared by his dance, Lynerkim pauses before his plunge to stare into the heavens. Gone are the pasted-on hair and eyebrows—now his giant skull gleams like a white marble bust, defenseless before this approaching thing even more awesome than he had imagined. A massive roiling ball of gas and rock cracking apart the sky! The fist of God! It echoes in his head like a roaring mob of singing angels serenading his last dance.

But Why Can No One Else See or Hear This Monstrous Thing?

Because it's not for them.

FILE: RETRIBUTION.

CPSIA information can be obtained
at www.ICGtesting.com
Printed in the USA
LVHW040851201120
672005LV00007B/460